Someone's Stalking Jamie . . .

Jamie reached Belmont Street. One more block to go.

Her shadow, long and thin, crossed the street ahead of her. A tree limb scratching loudly against the side of a house made her jump.

The tall hedge by the sidewalk shifted and rustled as if small animals were running up and down it. Her shadow glided ahead of her along the hedge, shifting and fading with the wind under the pale streetlights.

What was that?

Something strange was happening. Something different. Something not right.

She saw what it was.

Another shadow had joined hers on the hedge. Another shadow was gliding quickly toward hers.

She uttered a low cry, turned her head as she quickened her pace.

Yes. She was being followed.

Books by R. L. Stine

Fear Street: THE NEW GIRL
Fear Street: THE SURPRISE PARTY
Fear Street: THE OVERNIGHT
Fear Street: MISSING
Fear Street: THE WRONG NUMBER
Fear Street: THE SLEEPWALKER
Fear Street: HAUNTED
Fear Street: HALLOWEEN PARTY
Fear Street: THE STEPSISTER
Fear Street: SKI WEEKEND
Fear Street: THE FIRE GAME
Fear Street: LIGHTS OUT
Fear Street: THE SECRET BEDROOM

Fear Street Super Chiller: PARTY SUMMER

HOW I BROKE UP WITH ERNIE
PHONE CALLS
CURTAINS
BROKEN DATE

Available from ARCHWAY Paperbacks

BROKEN DATE

R.L. STINE

AN ARCHWAY PAPERBACK
Published by POCKET BOOKS
New York London Toronto Sydney Tokyo Singapore

This book is a work of fiction. Names, characters, places, and incidents are either the product of the author's imagination or are used fictitiously. Any resemblance to actual events or locales or persons, living or dead, is entirely coincidental.

An Archway Paperback published by
POCKET BOOKS, a division of Simon & Schuster Inc.
1230 Avenue of the Americas, New York, NY 10020

Published by arrangement with the author

ISBN: 0-671-69322-0

First Archway Paperback printing October 1991

10 9 8 7 6 5 4 3 2 1

Cover art by David Fishman

Printed in the U.S.A.

IL 6+

BROKEN DATE

1

Ouch!"

Jamie angrily tossed the magazine across the room and looked down at her index finger as a small line of bright red blood appeared. "I *hate* paper cuts!"

She sucked the blood off her finger, making a face at the bitter taste. Looking into the mirror for the two hundredth time that hour, she swept her straight black hair behind her shoulders, smoothing it with the hand that wasn't cut. For months, Jamie had wanted to get it cut stylishly short. But she couldn't. Tom liked it long.

Tom. She realized that she wasn't angry about the paper cut. She was angry about Tom. Where was he?

She looked again at the rainbow-colored Swatch on her wrist. Was it really five to two? Why do they make these trendy watches so impossible to read?

This wasn't at all like Tom. He was supposed to pick

her up at one to go skating at Forrest Rink. Now it was nearly two, and he hadn't shown up or called, or anything.

He had never done this before. In all the years they had been going together, he had never broken a date or arrived late without calling first. Good old reliable, dependable Tom.

So where was he?

Jamie sat down at her desk, then got up, then started pacing back and forth in her small room. She tripped over her skates and banged her knee hard against a bedpost. "Ouch!" If he didn't show up soon, she'd be bruised from head to foot!

She hobbled over to the white Formica desk, picked up her telephone and punched Tom's number. She let it ring six times, seven, eight—then replaced the receiver.

"Want to play a game?"

The voice made her jump. She spun around to see her ten-year-old brother Casey holding a game box in front of him.

"Don't you know how to knock?" Jamie snapped.

"Knock knock," Casey said. For a ten-year-old, he was a real wise guy. "Do you want to play?"

"No, thanks," Jamie said, checking her watch again.

"But it's a great game," Casey insisted, dropping it on her bed and starting to remove the box lid. "It's called Hungry Hippos. You see, you've got these hippos and you've got to make them eat marbles. What color hippo do you want?"

"I don't want to play!" Jamie screamed. "Can't you hear?"

Casey looked really hurt.

Jamie felt bad that she had yelled. It wasn't Casey's fault. "I'm sorry," she said quietly, putting a hand on his narrow shoulder. "I'm just upset because Tom was supposed to pick me up an hour ago, and he isn't here."

"Don't worry about him," Casey said, a devilish grin spreading across his dirty face. "He probably just went skating with somebody else!"

"Get out of here!" Jamie laughed, giving him a playful shove out the door. "You've got a rotten sense of humor."

"I wasn't kidding!" Casey insisted, grinning. Then he disappeared down the hall.

What a pest, Jamie told herself. He's such a perfect, pesty kid brother. He must take "kid brother" lessons after school or something.

She struggled to read her watch again. Nearly ten after two. The idea that Tom would go skating with someone else made her smile. They had been going together for so long—since junior high—they never had those insecure thoughts that troubled other couples they knew. Their life seemed so certain, so steady. They would both graduate from Cloverhill High in the spring. Then four years of college together up in Syracuse. Then they'd get married.

Their friends teased them and said they were already an old married couple. But they didn't mind. They both knew they were in love. They both knew they wanted to spend their lives together. It was so nice, so comfortable to have everything settled.

Jamie leaned against the dresser, stared into the mirror and applied fresh lipstick, the dark red lipstick Tom liked so much. Then she walked back to the desk and called his house again. Still no one home.

How long was she supposed to wait around?

She stared at the class portrait of Tom on her desk. She pointed a finger at him, at the amazing shock of white-blond hair that fell down his forehead. Some people thought he peroxided that front wave, it was so startlingly white. But that was its natural color. "So where *are* you?" she asked aloud.

She couldn't decide whether to be angry at him or to worry about him. So she decided to do both. She angrily tossed the skates into her closet. She slammed the closet door.

She went to the phone and dialed her best friend, Ann-Marie. "What are you doing?" she asked her.

"Talking to you on the phone," Ann-Marie said. Jamie had been best friends with Ann-Marie for three years and hadn't had a straight answer from her yet. She was as twisted as the red, curly hair that circled her round, freckled face. "Is that why you called? To ask me what I was doing?"

"No," Jamie said, not in the mood for her friend's kidding around. "I was bored."

"You were so bored you called me? Thanks for the compliment," Ann-Marie said. She had a husky, scratchy voice that made everything she said sound comical. "I'm bored, too."

"But you're always bored," Jamie said, and then laughed.

"Wow, you're full of compliments today. Weren't you supposed to go skating with Tom?"

"He stood me up," Jamie told her. The words sounded funny, as if someone else were saying them.

"We must have a bad connection," Ann-Marie said. "It sounded like you said Tom stood you up."

"He was supposed to pick me up at one," Jamie told her, sounding more upset than she had intended.

"Get off the phone. I have to call the *Courier-Herald.* This is front-page news!"

"I think I will get off the phone," Jamie said, regretting the call in the first place. She wasn't in the mood for Ann-Marie's jokes. "You're not cheering me up."

"Sorry. Do you want me to stand on my head?" Ann-Marie didn't give her a chance to reply. "Listen, Jamie, you've got to chill out. Didn't Tom have swim team practice this morning?"

"Yes, but—"

"Well, you know what a fanatic Coach Daniels is. He's probably keeping them all in the pool a few extra hours to see if they swim faster with wrinkly skin. I'm sure Tom couldn't get out of the pool to call you."

"Yeah. You're probably right," Jamie said reluctantly.

"You're gonna see him at the dance tonight anyway, right?"

"Yes, but—"

"I'll tell you what. Why don't you come to the mall

with me? It's too late to go skating anyway. We'll kill some time and maybe spend some money. Spending money always cheers me up. How about you? There are some new pink Reeboks I want to try on at Shoe World."

"Ann-Marie—*pink* Reeboks?"

"Yeah. They're on sale because the color is so disgusting. How about it? It'll take your mind off Tom. I promise."

Twenty minutes later, Jamie and Ann-Marie were walking through the Cloverhill Mall, crowded with Saturday afternoon shoppers. They stopped to look at a sky blue Camaro that was being raffled off by the Lions Club. "That's Tom's kind of car," Jamie said, reaching through the open window to feel the mock-leather seatcover.

"He can't afford roller skates."

"That's not funny, Ann-Marie. Tom won't be poor his whole life." Jamie glared at her friend. She didn't like people making fun of Tom because his family was poor.

"Touchy, touchy," Ann-Marie said, giving Jamie's long, black hair a playful tug. "You know I didn't mean anything. You're just upset because Tom broke your date."

They walked past a tiny store called Pop Art. A sign in the window boasted that they had twenty-two different flavors of popcorn, including peppermint and licorice. "Now that's really gross," Ann-Marie said. "Hey, there's Shoe World. Look, the pink

Reeboks are right in the window. That pink is really bright, huh? Coming in with me?"

"I don't think so," Jamie said. "I might go blind if I stand too close to them. You go ahead. I'll meet you over by The Record Rack."

Ann-Marie hurried to the busy shoe store. Jamie watched her for a while, then slowly began to walk toward the record store. She passed a fireplace store, a hardware store and a store with big, brawny male mannequins in the window, all wearing lumberjack outfits. But she didn't really see any of it. It was all a blur of pulsating lights and garish signs, people with blank faces, a steady stream of shopping bags and baby strollers that seemed to move in all directions at once.

She stopped in front of the Diamond Ranch, a jewelry store she had never noticed before. There was a display of antique stickpins in the window. She needed a birthday gift for her mother, she remembered, and these seemed to be to her mother's taste. They were on sale, too, so she went inside.

The store was long and narrow, with jewelry display cases on both sides, a narrow aisle in between. The door closed behind her and Jamie was startled by the sudden silence. Unlike most of the stores on this Saturday afternoon, the Diamond Ranch was empty.

She walked deeper into the store, looking from side to side into the display cases, past a case of gold chains, another of brass and silver loop earrings and another of pins and brooches of enamel birds. She smiled. There didn't seem to be any diamonds in the Diamond Ranch.

As she neared the back of the long store, the smile dropped from her face. She let out a silent gasp, stood frozen for a moment, then dropped to her knees behind a glass display case.

At first, she thought she was watching a TV show, or had maybe wandered onto the set of a movie.

But Jamie quickly realized that what she was seeing was real.

A few yards ahead of her at the back counter, a robbery was taking place. The store manager, a short, bald man with a very red face, stood with his back against the wall, his short arms raised high above his head. Every part of him seemed to be shaking, and he made a little whining sound with each quick breath he took.

A young man leaned against the counter, waving a small, silver pistol in the frightened manager's face. He banged the pistol handle hard on the glass display case and then gestured with it toward the cash register.

Jamie, too startled to breathe, too frightened to think or see clearly, stared at the back of the young man. She stared at the silver pistol, at his faded, blue denim jacket, at his white-blond hair.

His white-blond hair.

She let out a silent cry as she realized that the young man holding up the store was TOM.

2

Keeping low behind the jewelry case, Jamie stared through the glass at the back of Tom's head, at his broad shoulders as he gestured furiously with the pistol, and at the silver weapon as shiny as a jewel in his hand. Why is he doing this? she asked herself. How can he do this—to *us?*

She had a sudden impulse to jump up, to call out to him, to tell him to stop.

"Open the register. Hurry!" he yelled, glancing quickly to the front of the narrow store. His voice sounded different, strained, scared.

Jamie retreated until her back was against the wall. She ducked down lower behind the case. She knew she couldn't call out to him. She was too frightened, too shocked to move. She wanted to become invisible, just disappear.

Tom looked nervously around the store again, and she pulled back tighter against the wall. Her bag dropped out of her grasp. Her lipstick and a few other items spilled onto the floor. Her heart jumped. She grabbed the bag.

Had he heard?

No.

"Hurry it up, old man, or you're history!" he yelled in that fierce, frightened voice. He jabbed the barrel of the pistol into the little man's chest.

Jamie looked away. This wasn't happening. This was a bad dream. Wake up, girl. Wake up.

She stared into the case at a necklace of silver loops. As she gazed at it, the necklace began to change its shape. The loops shimmered before her, then blurred, then seemed to break apart and shatter into glowing pieces of dust.

Broken. Just like my life, Jamie thought.

The store manager's high-pitched shout snapped her back to reality. "You no-good punk!"

"Shut up! Shut up! Shut up!" Tom screamed, poking the old man's ribs with the pistol. "Empty the register—now!"

"That's all I got, punk," the little man said. His face had gone beyond red. It was as purple as a plum. "Did you hear me? You're a *punk!*"

Jamie cried out at the sound of the first pistol shot. It sounded like someone popping a paper bag in the lunchroom at school.

A bright circle of blood formed on the store manager's shirtfront. His dark face paled. His eyes grew wide in surprise.

With the sound of the second shot, he let out a low

moan. His hands gripped his chest, and he dropped heavily to the floor.

As Tom leaned over the counter to reach into the cash register drawer, Jamie leaped to her feet.

Would she be able to run? Would her legs work?

Yes. Grasping her bag tightly in one hand, she ran down the long aisle of the store, ran without breathing, without seeing, without looking back.

It seemed like a mile. It seemed like a hundred miles.

She pushed open the glass door and ran out of the store.

Did he see her? Did he recognize her?

She didn't wait to find out. Her heart pounding, the pop of the gunshots repeating again and again in her ears, she tried to hide in the blur of moving people as she hurried away from the jewelry store.

It felt good to be moving, to be part of a crowd. But she couldn't get the little man's look of surprise out of her eyes, couldn't get the strange sound of Tom's desperate voice from her ears.

Ahead of her, a little boy was crying. What was in his hand? Was it an ice-cream cone, an empty ice-cream cone?

"Look out!" a woman shouted.

Suddenly Jamie's right shoe slid out from under her, and she fell. "Ow!" she groaned, and realized she had stepped into the ice cream that had fallen from the little boy's cone. He started to cry even louder. His mother looked down at Jamie, offered a quick, "Sorry about that," and pulled the bawling kid away.

Aware of a crowd of people staring at her, Jamie started to pull herself up. "Hey, why didn't you give that kid his ice cream back?" Ann-Marie said, appearing from out of nowhere. She helped Jamie to her feet. "I can't take you anywhere, can I? Well, what do you think?" She pointed to the bright pink running shoes on her feet.

Jamie stared at the shoes, but couldn't say anything.

"You're speechless, right?" Ann-Marie said, pulling her away from the circle of ice cream on the tiled floor. "Well, I know they're a little more pink than most people would want, but they were such a bargain that I—" Ann-Marie suddenly realized that Jamie was very upset.

"Hey, don't sweat it. The ice cream will come off your shoe. It's only vanilla so it shouldn't be a problem. Did you hurt yourself when you fell?"

"I saw a robbery," Jamie blurted out.

"What?"

"I saw a robbery. In the Diamond Ranch." Saying the words gave Jamie chills down her back. She began to tremble violently.

"You look sick," Ann-Marie said, taking her arm. "Are you okay?"

"No," Jamie said, her voice a whisper.

"Uh . . . well . . . the Slurp Shop is right across the walk. Let's sit down and have a soda or something. Would that help?"

"No," Jamie said. "I think I want to go home."

Both girls looked toward the Diamond Ranch in time to see two concerned-looking mall security guards running inside, their hands on their gun holsters. They could hear the low whine of a siren in the distance.

"A man was shot," Jamie said, her voice shaking.

"And you saw it?" Ann-Marie asked, sounding more impressed than concerned. "Then, you're a witness. Don't you think you'd better stay and talk to the police?"

"No!" Jamie shouted, a bit too loudly. "I couldn't. I mean, I can't. I—maybe later. I've got to get home."

Should she tell Ann-Marie the most horrible part of all? Should she tell her that it was Tom who shot the store manager?

"Maybe you'll get in trouble for leaving the scene of a crime," Ann-Marie suggested. "Maybe it makes you an accessory or something. This is exciting!"

"You've been watching too many TV shows," Jamie muttered impatiently. "Come on, Ann-Marie. Are you going to take me home or not?"

Ann-Marie looked disappointed. "Okay. Of course. This way. The car is on the other side."

A few minutes later, Jamie collapsed onto the front seat of the Toyota and closed her eyes. Ann-Marie climbed behind the wheel and began to search her bag for the keys. "Do you think the man died?" she asked.

"Tom shot him twice. In the chest," Jamie said, her eyes still closed.

Ann-Marie dropped the keys onto the floor of the car. "Hey, are you okay? Maybe you're in shock or something. Did you hear what you just said? You just said *Tom* shot the guy."

Jamie was silent for a long time. "I know what I said," she told Ann-Marie finally. "It was Tom."

"Tom robbed the jewelry store? Tom killed the manager? Get real." Ann-Marie's words were as flip as ever, but the confidence had gone out of her voice.

Jamie opened her eyes. "I saw him. It was Tom. It was Tom. It was Tom. How many times do I have to say it before you'll believe me?"

"Okay, okay," Ann-Marie said, frowning. "You don't have to get angry with *me.*" She searched for the car keys under the seat. "It *is* a little hard to believe, you know."

"Yes," Jamie said, and tears filled her eyes. "Yes, it's hard to believe. But I saw him."

Ann-Marie started the car and backed out of the parking space. They rode in silence for a while as she maneuvered the car out of the vast mall parking lot. "Why would Tom rob a store? Where did he get a gun? Why would he do such a dumb thing? Why am I asking *you* these questions?" She reached a hand out and grabbed Jamie's shoulder. "I'm sorry. I guess I'm really upset, too."

"That's okay," Jamie said quietly. She didn't know what else to say. She was asking the same questions over and over again in her mind.

Sure, Tom's family was poor. His dad was one of the few blue-collar workers in Cloverhill. It was hard for Tom to fit into an upper-middle-class community like theirs. But he was good-looking, a great athlete and managed to make a lot of friends. Yes, he was always apologizing to Jamie for not having a car, for not being able to buy her expensive presents, for not being able to dress as stylishly as the other kids.

But he knew these things didn't matter to Jamie.

Didn't he?

"I don't know what to say," Jamie told her friend with a sigh. "I thought I knew everything about him."

"Wait a minute! Whoa!" Ann-Marie cried, screeching the car to a halt in Jamie's driveway. She jerked the gearshift into Park, then held a finger up in front of Jamie's face. "How many fingers do you see?"

"What?" Jamie was in no mood for silly games. Why couldn't Ann-Marie realize that?

"Come on, Jamie. How many fingers?"

"One. Why?"

"Were you wearing your glasses in the mall?"

"No," Jamie replied. "You know I never wear them when I go out. Too vain, I guess."

"So. There you have it. You're nearsighted, right?" Ann-Marie had a broad, triumphant grin on her face.

"Yeah. A little."

"So, you couldn't see clearly in the jewelry store. The guy only looked like Tom. But it wasn't Tom. That's the only logical explanation." She sat back in the seat and grinned at Jamie, very pleased with herself.

Jamie frowned and shook her head. "I wish I could believe you. . . ."

"But?"

"But it was Tom. Do you really think I wouldn't

know Tom? Do you really think I wouldn't recognize someone I know so well? I wouldn't need to see him clearly to know it was him."

Ann-Marie's smile faded, replaced by a thoughtful pout. "I guess you're right. I guess his white hair alone would give him away. You should tell him to wear a cap the next time he pulls a—" She stopped herself.

Jamie pushed open the car door.

"I'm sorry," Ann-Marie called after her. "I always make jokes. It's a defense mechanism, I guess. The more serious things are, the more hilarious I get. You should see me at a funeral. I'm a riot. But that doesn't mean I don't care."

"Talk to you later," Jamie said, wondering if her parents were home, wondering what she would say to them, wondering how much longer she could keep herself together without completely breaking apart.

"Call me," Ann-Marie said. "Really. Call me. You can always talk to me." She backed the car down the drive. She didn't sound her usual two honks as she drove away.

Jamie stood in the drive and watched Ann-Marie's car until it turned the corner and drove out of view. Then she slowly walked into the house, her mind whirling with horrible pictures, the sight and sounds of the holdup refusing to fade.

"Anybody home?"

There was no reply.

She found a note on the refrigerator, the usual place for messages and reminders. The note said that her parents had taken Casey to buy new shoes. That was good news. She really didn't feel like facing them at the moment.

She didn't feel like seeing anyone ever again.

She saw the green light flashing on the telephone answering machine. Someone had left a message. She pushed the button and waited for the tape to rewind.

She gasped aloud when she heard Tom's voice. She could hear a lot of noise and voices in the background. He must have been calling from a pay phone.

The first time the message played through, she didn't hear a word of it. When had he called her? she wondered. Before the robbery or after?

She had to rewind it and play it again. This time she forced herself to listen to the words: "Hi, Jamie. I hoped to catch you home. Uh . . . sorry about the skating. Daniels kept us in the pool till after two-thirty. Would you believe we had to practice breath control the whole time? I . . . uh . . . got to run. I have some . . . other things to take care of before the dance. Pick you up at eight. Hey, where *are* you, anyway? Bye."

Did he sound really nervous? Or was Jamie just imagining that?

No. His voice definitely sounded funny.

Was he calling from the locker room? From the mall? She played the message again. Again. She couldn't tell.

But he definitely sounded nervous. That she could tell.

She played it one more time, trying to decide if it was before the robbery or after. She stopped the message halfway through, a sudden chill running down her body.

Had he seen her as she ran out of the jewelry store? Was he pretending that he hadn't? Was he going to try to pretend that everything was normal, that everything was going to continue the way they had so carefully, so lovingly planned it?

Jamie put her head down on the kitchen counter. Her life had seemed so wonderful, so certain, so exciting just a few hours before. Now, it was all broken. All of the happy plans, all of their dreams, their whole life together. Broken.

She stood up straight and shook her head. How could she go to the stupid school dance with him tonight? No way!

He had ruined their life. And he had killed a poor, defenseless little man. She fought back a sudden wave of nausea. Her head felt light. Everything began to spin. Tom had killed a man. Now he was coming to take her to a school dance.

She steadied herself against the counter and picked up the phone receiver. She decided to call and break the date. She'd say she was sick. It was true, after all. She felt worse than sick. She felt like disappearing, dying.

The thought of his voice on the phone message, trying to sound so calm, so normal, made her feel even worse. There was no way she could face him.

She started to push his phone number, but stopped halfway through. She put down the receiver. I have to face him, she told herself. I have to know the truth.

Yes. It made a lot more sense to go to the dance with Tom. She would act as if nothing had happened. She would give him a chance to tell her all about what had happened, a chance to explain.

She owed him that much, after all.

She owed him for not realizing just how troubled he was, how unbalanced, how unhappy. She owed him the chance to explain.

This idea made her feel a little stronger. She glanced up at the kitchen clock above the sink. It was just about time to start getting ready. She hadn't planned on getting dressed up. No one ever did for dances in the high school gym. But she wanted to look nice. After all, it might be their last date together.

She picked up her bag and carried it to her bedroom. For some reason she found herself thinking about the tickets to the dance. She had bought them in homeroom Wednesday morning. But where had she put them?

In her wallet. She searched through the bag for the green leather wallet. Her feeling of dread grew as she continued to search.

Finally, desperately, she turned the bag over and dumped all of its contents onto her bedspread.

No wallet.

"Oh no," she moaned.

Had she dropped it in the jewelry store?

3

Hey, Jamie, Tom's here!"

Jamie heard Casey calling her from the living room, but of course, she already knew Tom was there. From her bedroom window, she had watched him walk up the drive, had already seen that he was wearing a new, pale blue sweater, that he was walking quickly, his head bobbing up and down to some melody inside his head, that he was wearing his usual smile.

How could he be smiling?

"Jamie," Casey repeated, a little louder, "Tom's here!"

Those words used to fill her with such happiness, such anticipation. Now she felt only dread.

She stopped at the top of the stairs. She suddenly felt as if she couldn't take another step. She wanted to turn around, to go back to her room, to climb into bed and pull the covers over her head.

"Hi, Jamie." Tom smiled up at her from the bottom of the stairs.

She couldn't turn around now. She tried to smile back at him, but her mouth wouldn't cooperate. "Hi," she said, trying to sound normal, but her voice sounded like someone else's.

"Please, just one game of Hungry Hippos," Casey whined, shoving the game box into Tom's chest.

"Sorry, Casey. I don't think we have time," Tom said, still smiling. He turned to Jamie. "Wow. You look great. Did you change your hair?"

That was a running joke with them because Jamie never changed her hair. She always wore it swept straight back behind her shoulders.

"Thanks," she said quietly, without smiling at his joke.

How could he act so normal?

"It doesn't take long to play," Casey insisted, shoving the box back into Tom's chest.

"Ouch!" Tom laughed and backed away. He ran his hand back through his wavy, white-blond hair. "I like your shirt. That's a great red," he told Jamie.

"Blouse, not shirt," she said, not meaning to sound as angry as she did. She quickly added, "It's silk. It's my mom's. She lent it to me."

She looked away. She stared at the stripes on the wallpaper. How many hours had she spent picturing his face, daydreaming about his face, staring at his picture? Now, it hurt to look at him.

"You didn't notice my new sweater." He sounded hurt. She always noticed things like that.

"Yeah. I did." She didn't feel like talking about sweaters. She felt like screaming, "Why did you murder a man this afternoon? Why did you ruin our lives?"

Tom looked nervous, too. Was he reading her thoughts?

They had been going together for so long, they often said the same things at the same time, often discovered they were silently sharing the exact same thought. Could he read her mind now? Did he know that she was there in the jewelry store? Did he know she had seen everything?

He pushed his hand through his hair again. He only did that when he was nervous or worried about something.

"We can play real fast," Casey insisted, putting the game box on the floor in the hallway and removing the lid. "I always cheat, so the game goes faster. Okay?"

"Well—" Tom seemed to be relenting.

"No!" Jamie screamed. "Leave us alone!" She didn't mean to scream. Get control, girl, she told herself. Get control now, or it's going to be a long evening.

Who was she kidding? It was going to be the longest evening of her life—and the saddest—no matter what.

Tom and Casey both looked at her, startled.

"Sorry," she said quietly to Casey.

"You okay?" Tom asked.

Okay? How could she be okay? How could he even pretend that everything was okay?

"Fine," she said, looking at the wallpaper. "Let's go."

"I guess I'll play by myself," Casey said with a shrug. He started banging away on the plastic hippos.

"Have a good time!" Jamie's mom called from the den.

If she only knew.

Everyone was acting so normally. And that made Jamie sadder than anything. Because she knew things would never be normal again.

She and Tom walked quickly out of the house and down the drive. It was a warm and humid night, too warm for the sweater Tom was wearing. Black clouds covered the moon. It felt as if it might rain soon.

"Step into my air car," Tom said, stopping at the sidewalk and pretending to open a car door for her.

His voice startled her. She was lost in her own sad thoughts. "Your what?"

"My air car. Some kids play air guitar. I drive an air car. It's not bad, huh?" He moved his hands around an imaginary steering wheel and pretended to drive. "Four on the floor. I get great mileage. And the stereo CD player is the greatest!"

Why was he fooling around like this? He didn't usually act so silly. He was definitely nervous, trying too hard, talking faster than usual, smiling a lot more.

"Maybe you should go back and play with Casey," she said coldly.

He grabbed his heart and groaned as if mortally wounded. "You don't like my air car? Okay. Then we'll have to walk, as usual."

When he grabbed his heart, she saw the little man in the jewelry store, saw the circle of blood growing on his shirtfront, saw him grab his chest and fall.

She looked at Tom, walking beside her, snapping his fingers to some silent tune, acting very nervous, very different, and she felt as if she were walking with a stranger. This couldn't be the same person she had felt so close to, the same person she had made so many wonderful plans with.

"Did you hear me?" His voice broke into her thoughts. "I said, you're very quiet tonight."

"Oh." She kept walking, looking straight ahead.

Jamie decided she couldn't go on with this. She couldn't pretend any longer. He had betrayed her. He had betrayed *them.* It was all broken. All of the feelings she had for him, all of the love. Broken. Gone.

What made her think she could go ahead with this date, pretend that everything was normal?

She decided to confront him right there on the street. Why drag it out? Why torture herself any longer?

He smiled at her, an awkward smile, a forced smile. He looked into her eyes, trying to determine what she was thinking. Despite her anger and hurt, she felt a rush of warm feeling for him.

This was no stranger. This was Tom.

Maybe he had an explanation.

She shook her head. What kind of explanation could there be for robbing a store, for killing a helpless man?

These thoughts spun through her mind, the conflicting feelings crashing against one another—first love, then anger, then a cold bitterness—until she thought she would scream. She had to stop and ask him about it. She had to know.

"Tom—" she started to say.

"Look, there's Alex and Sherry!" Tom cried, waving to their friends at the corner. "Wait up, you two!"

Sherry was wearing a pale blue Benetton sweater outfit. "Hey, we're twins!" Tom declared, holding the sleeve of his sweater up to hers. "You've got great taste in sweaters!"

Tom, Sherry and Alex had a good laugh about the sweaters. Alex suggested that Tom must have knitted his. Tom replied that the pale blue matched Alex's face. Alex shoved Tom off the sidewalk.

Jamie walked a few yards behind them. The more Tom kidded around, the worse she felt. And it was obvious, to her, at least, that he was kidding around a lot more than usual.

She knew that Tom didn't even like Sherry and Alex that much. They never hung out together or anything. But he had sure acted glad to see them tonight. It took all of Jamie's strength to keep walking behind them quietly, to keep from screaming to Tom to stop the foolish masquerade and admit to her what he had done.

Luckily it was just two more blocks to the high school.

When they got to the door, they were stopped at the ticket table by Mr. Seidendorfer, the music teacher. "Tickets, please," Mr. Seidendorfer hummed.

Tom, who had been telling a joke to Alex, turned back to Jamie. "Have you got the tickets?"

"Oh." The tickets. They were in her wallet, and her wallet was gone. "Uh . . . no. I don't."

Tom put a hand on her shoulder. It felt hot and wet over the silk blouse. "What's wrong with you tonight?" he asked, smiling.

How could he ask such a question?

"I don't know," was all she could say. "Sorry." She pulled away from him.

"Tickets, please," Mr. Seidendorfer repeated. Alex and Sherry had gone into the gym.

Jamie explained that she had lost her wallet with the tickets in it. Tom looked very embarrassed. Had he seen her wallet on the floor of the jewelry store? Mr. Seidendorfer considered it for a long moment, then motioned for them to go in.

"Did you really lose your wallet?" Tom asked.

"Yeah," Jamie said, looking around the gym to see who was there.

The gym had been decorated halfheartedly, a few balloons tied to the basketball hoops, a few droopy-looking red crepe streamers along the wall. It was hard to get kids to put in a lot of time decorating the gym for dances. Most couples would only stay at the dance for an hour or so anyway, and then leave to go to parties or drive around or hang out in town.

They walked around a bit, saying hello to some kids. They had to shout over the booming music, some sort of disco rap record that everyone was having trouble dancing to. The singer just kept repeating, "I don't wanna, I don't wanna, I don't wanna. . . ."

"Are you sure you're okay?" Tom shouted in her ear.

"What?"

"Are you okay?"

"I guess."

"Do you want to dance?"

That was about the last thing in the world she wanted to do. But she nodded her head yes. They walked to the center of the gym.

"I don't wanna, I don't wanna, I don't wanna. . . ."

At least, if they were dancing, he'd stop asking her if she was okay. At least, she wouldn't have to pretend to keep up a conversation. They started to dance, struggling to pick up the odd, jerky beat.

"I don't wanna, I don't wanna. . . ."

Suddenly Tom stopped, grasped her hand tightly in his hot, wet hand and began to pull her toward the far door. "I have to talk to you," he shouted.

He looked very worried. Or was she imagining that?

She didn't resist. She let him pull her toward the exit. Yes, he was definitely nervous. Otherwise, why was his hand so sweaty? He was usually cool as a cucumber.

This is it, Jamie thought. Here comes the worst moment of my life.

No. Here comes the *second* worst moment. The first was when I saw him in the jewelry store.

"Hey, Tom, where ya goin'?" someone yelled.

Tom ignored the voice. He pushed open the gym

door and pulled her into the dimly lit corridor. The door closed behind them, and the deafening music was reduced to a throbbing thump-thump-thump of bass and drums.

"Where shall we go?" Tom asked, still gripping her hand tightly in his. "Oh. I know." He walked a few doors down the long, empty hallway and pushed open the door to the woodworking shop. It was dark and cool in the shop. A single bulb on the far wall provided the only light.

Tom let go of Jamie's hand and began to pace back and forth in front of the workbenches, his hands in his pockets. Jamie felt a sudden chill. It was so dark in here, and he was acting so strangely.

She heard footsteps out in the hall, some giggling. The gym door was opened, allowing a few notes of loud music to escape. Then the door closed. The shop was silent again, silent except for the scrape of Tom's shoes against the concrete floor as he paced.

He stopped at the wall suddenly and picked a tool off a rack. It looked to Jamie like some sort of pick. Holding it in his left hand, he began to slap the blade against the palm of his right hand.

"Tom?" she called, her throat suddenly choked with fear.

He didn't seem to hear her. He slapped the blade of the pick against his palm, softly at first, then harder.

"Tom? What is it you want to tell me?"

He looked up at her. What was that look on his face? Was he glaring at her angrily? Was that a menacing stare, a look of absolute hatred? It was so hard to tell. He was completely hidden in shadow. She could barely see him. She could only see the glint of the pick blade and hear the slap-slap-slap of it against his palm.

Jamie had been angry at him all night, but now her emotion had changed. She felt fear, cold fear. She realized that she was frightened of this boy she thought she loved, this boy she thought she knew so well.

"I—I guess I'm a little nervous," he said, his voice tight. He slapped the pick blade against his hand. He took two steps toward her.

"What?" She couldn't think of anything to say. She wanted to back away, to run out the door, to get to the safety of the crowded, noisy gym.

He took another step toward her. What did he want? What was he going to do with that pick? Was he planning to threaten her? Was he planning to kill her because she saw him shoot the jewelry store manager?

No! That was impossible—wasn't it?

Not Tom.

He took another step toward her. He was right in front of her now. She stared down at the pick in his hand, watched it slap against his open palm.

"Jamie, I'm sorry. But I have to—"

He had the strangest, most awful look on his face.

Oh, no. It's broken. All broken, Jamie told herself. Something inside her had snapped, broken apart. Something had fallen away, had allowed all of her panic to escape, to flood her mind, to capture her, to swallow her up.

It was the look on his face, so nervous, so *guilty.*

It was the slow, determined way he approached her, step by step.

It was the slap-slap-slap of the blade.

"No!" Jamie screamed. "No!"

She had held herself in for so long. It felt good to scream, to let it all out. All of the anger, all of the disbelief, all of the terror came pouring out at once.

"How could you? How could you ruin our lives?"

Tom looked stunned. He took a step back.

But he wasn't fast enough.

She grabbed the pick from his hand.

"You've ruined everything!"

She stabbed it deep into his chest. Again. Again.

"Jamie, *no!*"

He grabbed at his chest and fell to the floor.

Jamie dropped the blood-covered pick to the floor beside him. Then she turned, pushed open the door and ran out into the corridor.

"I killed him! I killed him!" she screamed.

4

"I killed him! I killed him!"

Jamie's voice echoed off the tile walls as she ran down the empty corridor. She ran past a blur of green lockers, past the gym with the thump-thump-thump of drums vibrating the double doors, past a startled couple who had to leap out of her way.

"Please help me! I killed him!"

Turning a corner, she stumbled on the newly waxed floor and fell. Her knee hit hard, and the pain shocked her into silence.

"Jamie, what's the matter?"

Was it really Ann-Marie?

Yes. Ann-Marie slowly came into focus. She still had her jacket on. She was wearing a denim skirt. Jamie didn't remember ever seeing her in anything but jeans or cords.

"Help me. Please," Jamie moaned, still on her knees on the floor.

"What's wrong?" Ann-Marie cried, hurrying over to her and bending down to help her to her feet. "Did you fall?"

Ann-Marie looked up at Tom, who came running up behind Jamie. "Tom, what's going on?"

Tom shrugged. "I don't know. We were in the shop. I started to talk to her. Suddenly she screamed and ran out."

Ann-Marie looked skeptical. "Are you sure that's all that happened?"

"Yes. Of course I'm sure," Tom insisted. He started to take Jamie's arm, but she pulled away from him.

Jamie was on her feet now. She struggled to focus. "I—uh—" She turned to Tom and stared at the front of his shirt.

No blood. No wound. He was perfectly okay.

"Jamie, what happened?" Ann-Marie asked impatiently as she waved down the hall to Buddy Miller, her date, signaling to him that she'd be right there.

"I don't know," Jamie said, unable to take her eyes off Tom's shirtfront. "I guess I had some sort of daydream or something. I—"

Suddenly Jamie felt terribly embarrassed.

How could she have imagined stabbing Tom? Had she become so upset, so frightened that she lost her grip on reality?

Or was she hallucinating the Tom standing next to her? Was the real Tom lying in a pool of blood back in the dark woodshop?

She reached out and grabbed his arm. No. This Tom was real. Tom was alive, staring into her eyes, trying to figure out what had just happened. The stabbing was not real.

"Tom, I'm so sorry—" she started.

But then she saw the shiny blade in his hand. He was still carrying the pick. Why? Had he chased her down the hall with it? Did he plan to use it on her?

A cold chill ran down her back. She uttered a short cry and lurched away from him.

"Jamie, are you sick?" Ann-Marie asked, putting an arm around her shoulder.

"No. I—uh—yes." She felt terribly confused. Her head felt heavy, the way it did when she had been studying for four hours straight. Her eyes refused to focus.

Ann-Marie glared at Tom accusingly. He shrugged again. "She seemed fine when I picked her up," he said.

"I think I'd better go home. I'm really sorry," Jamie said softly, staring at the yellow wall.

"Okay, fine. I'll take you home," Tom said, reaching for her hand. "Can you walk okay?"

"No!" Jamie cried, pulling away from him.

"I think you've done enough already," Ann-Marie told him bitterly.

His face, pale in the dim yellow light, filled with confusion. The tool fell from his hand and bounced across the floor. He didn't try to pick it up. He stood staring at Jamie, as if waiting for an explanation.

"Tom, I think you'd better go. I'll take Jamie home," Ann-Marie said.

"Now, wait a minute. What's going on?" Tom

sounded more angry than hurt. "I can take care of Jamie."

Something about the way he said those words sent another chill down Jamie's back. She shivered.

"I can take care of Jamie."

Was this the boy she had been so close to for so long? Was this the boy she planned to marry? What had happened? Had he changed so much overnight? Or had she just never realized what he was really like? How had he been able to fool her for so long?

"Good night, Tom," Jamie said, looking beyond him down the corridor. "I really would like Ann-Marie to take me home."

Tom opened his mouth in protest. But no words came out. He looked at her, a pleading look, a hurt look. Then when she didn't respond, when she kept staring past him, not seeing him at all, not seeing anything, he turned, kicked the tool as hard as he could down the hall and stomped angrily away.

"What happened?" Ann-Marie whispered as they watched him disappear around the corner. "Did he admit it? About the robbery?"

"No," Jamie said, shivering again.

Ann-Marie pulled off her jacket and slipped it around Jamie's shoulders. It was too small for Jamie. It slipped off immediately. She pulled it back on. It warmed her a little.

"Well, what did he say?" Ann-Marie asked, still whispering even though no one was around.

"Nothing," Jamie snapped, annoyed. She didn't

feel like answering questions. Besides, what was there to say? Tom hadn't admitted anything. He hadn't said anything. He had just paced back and forth nervously, and then he had come toward her with that strange look on his face, with that horrid pick in his hand.

Ann-Marie held Jamie's arm and stared at her, waiting for her to say something. "Hey, Ann-Marie, come on! They're playing our song!" Buddy yelled from the door to the gym.

Both girls listened for a moment. The song pounding through the open gym door was "Fight for Your Right to Party" by the Beastie Boys.

"That's your song?" Jamie cried, making a face.

"Yeah. Buddy's very romantic," Ann-Marie replied.

Jamie laughed. Ann-Marie could always make her laugh, no matter what.

"Listen, I'll go get the car keys from Buddy and tell him I'm driving you home. We can talk on the way, if you want to. Okay?"

Jamie smiled and nodded yes.

As Ann-Marie jogged down the hall to Buddy, Jamie examined her knee. There was a small bruise, but the painful throbbing had stopped. She was starting to feel a little better. Her heartbeats had slowed to their normal pace, and her head didn't feel so heavy.

I feel better because Tom left, she told herself.

What a terrible thing to think. But it was true.

She had been truly terrified of him, so terrified that she had hallucinated stabbing him, so terrified that she must have gone out of her mind for that brief moment.

Did she have reason to be so terrified? Or was that caused by her crazy imagination too?

No. No, she told herself. She wasn't completely crazy. She had good reason to be afraid. Hadn't she seen him shoot that defenseless store manager twice?

She looked down the hall, eager to leave, eager to get back to the safety of her room. But even her bedroom would offer no safety now, no safety from her thoughts, no safety from the fact that her life was ruined, all of her plans, all of her dreams ended.

Down the hall, Ann-Marie seemed to be having some sort of argument with Buddy. He pulled her into the gym, and the door closed behind them. Jamie felt embarrassed. What was Ann-Marie telling Buddy? Jamie didn't want anyone to know what had happened. She didn't want anyone to think she was nuts or something. And she didn't want anyone feeling sorry for her.

Word would get around school soon enough that she and Tom were having troubles. And then when the police caught up to Tom and everyone found out that he had robbed a store and killed a man, then—

Then, what?

What would people think of her? What would people say to her? How could she face anyone ever again?

"Hey, snap out of it!" Ann-Marie was jingling the car keys in front of Jamie's face. "You in a trance, or what?"

"No. Oh. Sorry." Jamie shook her head, trying to shake away her thoughts.

"You feeling any better? You look a little less green. Of course, everyone looks like green slime under those ridiculous yellow lights!"

Jamie laughed. "Yeah. I'm feeling better. A lot, actually."

"Good. Let's go," Ann-Marie said, starting toward the front exit.

"Listen, Ann-Marie, why don't you stay here? Go dance with Buddy."

"But what about you? I—"

"I'm feeling fine now. Really. I'm perfectly okay. A little fresh air and I'll be completely back to normal. Whatever that means." She forced a smile. "I really don't feel like talking. I'd just like to walk home by myself. You know, have a little time to sort things out."

"Well . . ." Ann-Marie looked into her eyes, as if trying to determine if she really was feeling all right. "Are you sure you'll be okay?"

"Sure," Jamie said, squeezing Ann-Marie's hand. "Thanks a lot. You're always there when I need you."

"Well, if you want to talk later . . ."

"Thanks," Jamie said gratefully. "It's been a rough day. I just need some time to think."

"Okay. Take it easy." Ann-Marie turned and headed back to the gym.

A few moments later, Jamie stepped out the door into the dark coolness of the night. A strong wind had blown in from the east, and it rippled the hedges that bordered the school grounds and caused the old oaks and sycamores that lined the sidewalk to whisper and bend.

Jamie took a deep breath. She recognized the sweet aroma of apple tree wood. The Fawcetts who lived next door to the high school had cut down their apple tree a few weeks before. Now they must be burning the pungently sweet wood in their fireplace.

Jamie smiled. There was something so warm and comforting about the wonderful aroma, about walking past these familiar houses, down this familiar street to the house she had always lived in.

Some things stay the same, she decided. Even when your life is broken, even when all of your plans are torn apart, some things stay the same.

She crossed Hoople Street and turned right on Vermont. A car went past slowly and honked its horn. It was two kids she knew, either late for the dance or just cruising around town. She waved and kept walking.

A rattling sound in the street startled her. In the light of the streetlight, she saw that it was just a flattened tin can being blown by the wind.

She began walking faster. The wind was probably bringing a storm with it. A whistling gust blew over the trash can beside the Feldons' house. Trash poured out and the lid rolled down the driveway as if trying to escape.

She reached Belmont Street. One more block to go.

Her shadow, long and thin, crossed the street ahead

of her. A tree limb scratching loudly against the side of a house made her jump.

The tall hedge by the sidewalk shifted and rustled as if small animals were running up and down it. Her shadow glided ahead of her along the hedge, shifting and fading with the wind under the pale streetlights.

What was that?

Something strange was happening. Something different. Something not right.

She saw what it was.

Another shadow had joined hers on the hedge. Another shadow was gliding quickly toward hers.

She uttered a low cry, turned her head as she quickened her pace.

Yes. She was being followed.

5

Watching the shadow on the hedge, Jamie walked even faster, her shoes clicking loudly on the sidewalk. Her forehead began to ache. She could feel her fear grip her throat and wondered if she'd be able to scream for help if she had to.

The shadow began moving faster too, gliding silently along the shifting, rustling hedge. Its head was bent forward, its long, thin arms swung rapidly back and forth, almost as if swimming.

Jamie felt as if she were swimming, too. Her eyes blurred as if underwater. She gulped for air. The wind seemed to push her back, like ocean waves.

Why hadn't she accepted Ann-Marie's offer? Why did she insist on walking home?

She just hadn't been able to think clearly since . . . since the sight of the holdup in the jewelry store, since seeing Tom with that gun, since seeing him shoot the little man. She hadn't been able to think clearly, or to think of anything else.

She started to run. The shadow began to run, too. The two shadows were nearly side by side on the hedge.

Suddenly, the hedge ended. But the soft thud of running footsteps behind her continued. She was almost home, just three houses to go.

Just three houses to go. Now two. Then she had a terrifying thought: what if she were imagining this, too?

What if no one was chasing her?

What if her mind was betraying her again?

She had to find out. She had no choice.

Her legs aching, her forehead throbbing with pain, she reached her driveway. Then she spun around suddenly, almost losing her balance, and stared back at her pursuer.

She saw a blur of pale blue and white. Whoever it was leaped behind a tree.

Someone was there. For a brief moment, she felt strangely relieved. Better to be chased by a real person than by your own mind running wild.

Then the fear came rushing back. She forced her legs to carry her up the driveway. The porch light was on, but the rest of the house was dark. Her parents must be in the den in back. She was only a few yards from the front stoop now. Would the door be open?

She turned again, and saw the figure dive back into twisting tree shadows.

"Tom?"

Had she seen the flash of that white hair reflected in the streetlight?

"Tom?"

Her voice was a whisper on the wind. She tried to shout louder, but her heart was beating too fast, her throat too choked and dry to cooperate.

"Tom? Is that you?"

A gust of wind was her only reply. Shadows shifted on the lawn. No figure emerged from the darkness. A cat howled down the block, sounding horribly human, like a screeching child.

Jamie wanted to howl, too. She wanted to screech at the top of her lungs.

"Tom? Why are you doing this? Is that you?"

Silence. The cat wailed again.

"Do you want to talk?"

Silence.

She reached for the front doorknob with a trembling hand, turned it and pushed the door in. Stepping into the house, she took one more look back into the shadowy front yard. He was running away now, running toward the street, head low, running in a crouch, staying in the shadows, trying not to be seen.

But she could see his hair. His white hair.

She stood at the doorway and watched until the darkness swallowed him up. Then she closed the door and locked it. She leaned back, trying to catch her breath, pressing her back hard against the door as if trying to keep the outside out.

She closed her eyes and took a deep breath, then

another. With her eyes closed, she again saw the shadows racing against the hedge, then the crouching figure running to the street.

Her mind swirled with a hundred questions. Why did Tom follow her? Why did he chase her and then hide in the shadows? Was he afraid to face her? Was he afraid to tell her his terrible secret, the secret she already knew?

Or worse, much worse: Was he trying to frighten her?

"Jamie, what's wrong? Why are you home so early?"

Jamie opened her eyes and stepped away from the door. "Hi, Mom."

"Who is it, Shirl?" Jamie's dad, the newspaper in his hand, came hurrying into the room.

"It's Jamie. She's home already."

"You scared us," her dad said. "We were in the den. We heard a noise."

"Sorry," Jamie said, still trying to calm down.

He turned and went back to finish reading his newspaper. "You look terrible," her mother said, pulling on Jamie's jacket sleeve. "You're positively green. Are you sick?"

"No, Mom. I—"

"Do you have a temperature? I don't like your eyes. Those are sick eyes. Have you got the flu? Where's Tom? I didn't hear him leave."

Jamie's mother was a short, chubby woman with a round, lively face topped by frizzy blond curls. Once she got started asking questions, it was hard to get her to stop. She was like a bee, always hovering around you just a little too closely, fluttering off for a second or two, then flying right back at you, prodding and buzzing away more insistently than before.

"I'd better take your temperature. I've never seen you this pale. You're green. Absolutely green. Stick out your tongue. No. Don't stick out your tongue. Just tell me your symptoms. Are you queasy? You look like you might be queasy."

Normally, this kind of treatment from her mother drove Jamie over the edge. But she was so relieved to be home and safe, so relieved to be out of the shifting shadows, away from her silent pursuer, that she smiled.

"I'm feeling much better, Mom," she said, her voice still unsure. "The dance was a drag. I wasn't feeling too well, and Tom—uh—he was exhausted from swim practice. So we just decided to call it a night."

Her mother eyed her suspiciously. "You don't look right to me. I know when you're not right. How about some tea? Tea is good for when you're queasy."

"I'm not queasy, Mom. Really. But okay. I'll take a cup of tea."

"You must be queasy. When do you ever drink tea if you're not queasy?"

Jamie laughed. She stepped forward and hugged her mother. She had to bend down to reach her.

"Now I *know* you're sick," her mother said, smiling. Showing affection always embarrassed her. "Go away. Let me fix you some tea. Go upstairs. I'll bring it up to you."

"Mom, really, that isn't necessary."

"You're green. You're absolutely green."

"Okay, okay. I'm going."

She climbed up to her room, grateful that Casey had a sleep-over date at his friend Max's. Otherwise, he'd probably be after her to play Hungry Hippos or something. She really didn't think she could handle Hungry Hippos now.

She changed into her nightshirt and dutifully drank the tea her mother brought her. It felt warm and soothing, although she realized it would take more than a cup of tea to make her feel better.

Her mother hovered about, making small talk, asking about the dance, eyeing her suspiciously, commenting on her greenness until the last drop of tea had disappeared.

All the while, a voice kept repeating in Jamie's ear, "Tell her. Tell her about Tom, about the holdup, the shooting."

It would be so easy after this, the worst day of her life, to turn into a little girl and tell her mother everything, to share the horror of it all, to share her sadness, her utter despair. But each time the urge nearly brought her to telling her mother, she held herself back with the words "It isn't fair."

It wouldn't be fair to her mother to have the whole crazy story dumped on her like a ton of garbage. What could her mother do? Worry for Jamie? Panic for Jamie?

No, it wouldn't be fair. Not yet, anyway.

And it wouldn't be fair to Tom, either.

Fair to Tom? Why should she be fair to Tom? Hadn't he come after her with a pick? Hadn't he followed her home? Hadn't he tried to scare her to death?

Hadn't he shot a man? Shot a man? Shot a man? Shot a man?

"Jamie, what's wrong?"

"Nothing, Mom. Sorry. I was just thinking about something."

"You were just staring at me for the longest time. I think you're sicker than you're letting on. Go on. Get into bed. I'll tuck you in."

"What?"

"I said, I'll tuck you in. What is it, Jamie? What's troubling you?"

"Nothing, Mom. Really. You're right. I just don't feel right. I'll tuck myself in. Okay? Good night. I'll be fine in the morning. Really."

Her mother circled around a few more times before going downstairs. She pulled back the covers, tossed Jamie's dirty clothes into the laundry hamper and dusted off the desk lamp shade with her hand. Then she gave Jamie one last concerned look, tossed her a kiss with her pudgy little hand and fluttered out of the room.

As soon as her mother had gone downstairs, Jamie sank onto the bed. She closed her eyes and thought about sleep. She knew she had to be exhausted from all that had happened during that long, horrifying day. But she didn't feel the least bit tired. Sleep was still a long way away.

She lay in bed, her light still on, staring up at the ceiling. She knew what she had to do. But would she do it?

Yes.

She jumped up, walked over to the phone and pushed Tom's number.

She let it ring six times before she hung up.

Tom must not have been back yet. But where was his mother? She knew that Tom's dad was on a trip upstate. His mother wouldn't go out on a Saturday night without him.

Strange . . .

Jamie decided that maybe she had dialed the wrong number. She pushed it again, this time concentrating on her finger as it hit each number.

It rang and rang. No. No one home.

She slowly replaced the receiver and started back toward her bed. She yawned, suddenly feeling very sleepy.

The phone rang.

She grabbed it up before the first ring had ended. "Is that you, Tom?"

The voice on the other end sounded distant and muffled. "I'm sorry you saw me at the mall," it said. "I'm real sorry."

6

Tom, is that you?"

Silence on the other end.

"Why do you sound so strange?"

"I'm real sorry," the muffled voice repeated.

"Tom, where are you? I tried your house and there was no answer."

"Now I have no choice." His voice was soft but threatening. He talked very slowly.

Was this a dream?

No.

She looked around the room. Everything was as it always had been. She felt the phone receiver against her ear. It wasn't a dream.

Jamie could feel the terror take over her entire body. Her trembling hand began to pulse with pain. She realized she was squeezing the phone too tightly.

"Tom, what are you saying? Do you want to talk?"

Silence.

"Why do you sound so weird? What do you mean you have no choice?"

Silence.

"It's me—Jamie—remember? You can always talk to me, about anything. That's what you've always said. You've always said I'm the best listener in the world. So give me a chance, Tom. Let me listen. Let me know why you sound so strange, why you're trying to frighten me."

She realized she was babbling now. The terror had taken over from her brain. Her words were coming out in choked whispers. She didn't really hear what she was saying.

She just wanted a word from him. A soft word. A familiar word. A word to let her know that he was still Tom, still the boy she knew so well, still the boy she loved.

But there was only silence at the other end.

Then his voice repeated, this time forcefully, "I have no choice."

She tried to plead with him, but her throat tightened. No sound came out.

She heard a soft click.

"Tom, no! Don't hang up!" she managed to say.

But the line was dead.

She sat listening to the silence, to the soft crackle of the empty line. His last words repeated in her ear until they formed an angry chant.

"I have no choice. No choice. No choice."

"He wants to kill me," she told herself. "Tom wants to kill me because I saw him in that store."

But that didn't make any sense.

No sense at all.

Tom loved her. She loved Tom.

It isn't Tom, she thought. It's someone else.

It's a stranger who wants to kill me.

That frightening thought cheered her.

Better to be threatened by a stranger than by the boy you loved.

She hurled the phone to the floor, suddenly realizing the absurdity of her thoughts.

I'm going crazy, she thought. My brain is out of control.

I've got to be sensible. That's what everyone always tells me I am. Sensible. Now I've got to prove that they're right. I've got to calm down. Be sensible. I've got to think.

The phone was wailing at her feet, that annoying siren when it's been left off the hook. Frowning, she picked it up and replaced it.

She had an idea.

Time for a little detective work. Time to do a little checking. A little sensible thinking. A little sensible checking.

She fumbled around on the desk for her address book, and then searched through it for Andy Freed's phone number. Andy was Tom's best friend. And he was co-captain of the swim team.

She began to push Andy's number.

Was it too late to call?

Who cared? Her life had just been threatened and she was worrying about how late it was!

That's being a little too sensible, she told herself.

The phone rang twice and then was picked up. "'Lo?"

"Andy?"

"Yeah."

"Hi, it's Jamie. How are you?"

"Jamie? Aren't you out with Tom?"

"No. Well, I was. I mean, I wasn't feeling well so I came home early. Listen, Andy, I—"

"I had to stay home and baby-sit Kimberly. Some thrill, huh?" Andy said. "There wasn't anything on TV, and I had to play Candyland with her all night. Would you believe she's still awake?"

"What a bummer," Jamie said, impatient to get past the small talk. "I'm calling because . . . uh . . . I just wanted to ask you something."

"Yeah?"

"Was Tom at swim practice this afternoon?" Please, please say yes, she thought.

"Yeah, he was," Andy said. "But he left early, I think."

Oh, no, Jamie thought. No, no, no, no.

"What do you mean you *think?*" Jamie asked, holding on to every last shred of hope.

"Kimberly, shut up!" Andy shouted. "Sorry," he told her. "I don't know where she gets her energy. Maybe she's hyperactive or something. My luck, huh?"

"What do you mean you think Tom left early?" Jamie repeated, unable to hide her impatience.

"Well, I didn't see him when I got dressed after

practice," Andy said. "I mean, he wasn't in the locker room. So I guess he left early. Hey, are you two having trouble, or something?"

"No. No trouble," Jamie said, her voice a whisper. "Thanks, Andy. Bye." She hung up quickly.

No trouble.

No trouble at all.

Tom had lied to her about staying late at swim practice. He had left early, had gone to the mall, had held up a jewelry store, had killed the owner.

No trouble. Thanks, Andy. Thanks, Tom.

Jamie didn't feel like being sensible anymore.

She climbed into bed and pulled the covers up over her head. She wanted to hide, to disappear in the darkness, silent and alone . . . forever.

7

I can explain it all to you," Tom said.

She sat up and rubbed her eyes. Her neck ached. She must have been sleeping in an awkward position. "What time is it?" she asked, her voice husky, still sleep-clogged.

"It doesn't matter," he said. "I can explain it all." His eyes seemed to glow, seemed to light up her dark bedroom. Moonlight through the open window made his white hair sparkle.

"But what are you doing here? How did you get in?"

He came up close and grabbed her hand. He grinned a preposterously wide grin. "It doesn't matter. Nothing matters. I can explain everything."

He began to pull her out of bed, first softly, then with more force when she resisted. "No, wait, Tom. Where are you taking me?"

His eyes glowed fiery red. He suddenly looked like some sort of a demon to her. His grin grew wider, as if it would swallow his entire face. "I want to explain it all, Jamie. I can explain everything."

He was pulling her to the window.

"I want you to understand," he said, still grinning. "I don't want you to be upset with me."

"But where are we going?" she asked, tugging out of his grasp.

"I'll show you. Get dressed."

A few seconds later she was dressed. They were out her bedroom window, then driving in a car she'd never seen before, then walking in the night chill in a neighborhood she'd never visited.

"I want to explain it all," Tom repeated. Now his eyes glowed royal-blue, then purple, and the moon made his slicked-back white wave of hair look as hard as a statue's.

"But where are we?" she asked, already filled with doubt, already sorry she'd agreed to sneak out and accompany him to this strange neighborhood of run-down, low buildings and garbage-strewn walks, of narrow, cluttered alleys, and open windows with loud, unfamiliar music blaring.

"You'll see," he whispered, grinning like a panting dog. "You'll see."

They stopped at the doorway to an all-night cafeteria. Inside, the lights were bright, almost too bright, a white light that made her close her eyes and turn her head. "Here we are," he said.

His grin wasn't at all familiar to her. Something about him had changed. In fact, everything about him had changed. "Who are you?" she asked.

He placed a finger on her lips to silence her.

They peered through the smeared glass doorway into the cafeteria. The little man at the cashier's counter was the only person there. The chairs were all upended on the long rows of tables. The food had all been put away.

"Let's go in. I can explain," Tom said, squeezing her arm. He'd never squeezed her arm that way before.

"I really don't want to," she said, pulling back as he slid open the door.

He looked hurt. "But I want to explain. I need to explain."

She followed him into the cafeteria. They walked up to the cashier's counter. Jamie gasped. The little man counting a stack of bills behind the cash register looked so much like the manager at the Diamond Ranch.

"I can explain," Tom said. She saw for the first time that he had a shiny silver pistol in his hand. He handed it to her and pulled another pistol from his denim jacket.

She stared at the pistol in her hand. It felt hot and moist from his palm. "No," she said. "Please, Tom. I don't want to do this."

A grin was his only reply.

She tried to put the pistol back in his hand, but he stepped away from her and walked up to the cashier. The little man looked up from his stack of bills, saw the pistols and raised his hands high above his head. Money fluttered to the floor.

"Tom, don't!" she cried.

He raised the pistol and pointed it at the little man's chest. "I can explain everything," he said, looking at the quivering, terrified cashier.

"Well, okay," she said impatiently. "Go ahead. Explain. I've been waiting all this time. Explain it. Please. Please explain it."

"I can," he said. He waited a long time, the gun trained on the little man with his hands in the air. "You see, I'm tired of being poor."

His words hit her like a bullet.

"That's it? That's how you explain it?"

He grinned at her. "Yes. I told you I could explain everything."

Then he pulled the trigger.

She awoke and sat up in bed, still feeling the chill of the dream. Tom's glowing demon eyes and grin took a long time to fade.

What a nightmare!

If only the real nightmare could fade away with the dream.

Her neck ached. She tried to rub the soreness out of it. The muscles felt hard and tight. As she rubbed, she glanced up at the clock on her desk. Eleven o'clock Sunday morning. Her parents had let her sleep late.

They must have been really worried about her. She guessed she had really looked a sight the night before.

She pulled on jeans and a pale blue sweatshirt without seeing them. She pulled a hairbrush through her hair twice. Then she hurried downstairs, taking the stairs two at a time.

"Did Tom call?" she asked, bursting through the swinging kitchen doors. She realized she probably should have said good morning first, shouldn't have sounded so eager, so desperate.

"Good morning to you, too," her mother said dryly. "How do you feel?" Her mother buzzed over and put a hand under her chin, examining Jamie's face. The hand was wet from washing breakfast dishes. "Still got those circles around your eyes. Did you sleep well? Are you still so queasy?"

"Shirl, give the girl a break," Jamie's father said from behind his newspaper. He was at his usual place at the kitchen table, sections of the newspaper scattered all around, a half-chewed English muffin still on his plate.

"A break? What kind of a break?" her mother asked, going back to the sink. "A girl comes home early from a dance sick as a dog, and I'm not supposed to be a little concerned?"

"I wasn't sick as a dog," Jamie insisted wearily.

"You don't have to twist her head off to see if she has rings under her eyes."

"How would you know what I'm doing? You don't take your nose out from behind that newspaper."

"She didn't twist my head off," Jamie said quietly. "Did Tom call?"

"He didn't call," her mother said. "He was here."

Everything flashed white. Jamie felt her heart leap. "He was here?"

"Eight-thirty this morning. I was up, but your

father was still asleep," her mother said, carelessly sponging off dishes and putting them in the dishwasher. "What's going on with you two, anyway?"

"Nothing," Jamie said, much too loudly to be convincing. "What did he say? What was he doing here?"

Her father lowered his newspaper to look at her.

Yes, she was acting strangely. But she couldn't help it.

She smiled at him. It wasn't a very convincing smile, but it was the best she could do.

"He left a package for you," her father said, pointing to a small, gift-wrapped box on the kitchen counter.

"He said it was a present for you. He said he wanted you to have it as soon as you woke up," her mother said, wiping her hands on a dish towel. "Isn't that sweet?"

Jamie hurried to the counter and grabbed the little box. "Is that all he said? Did he leave a note? Did he say where he was going?"

Again, her father lowered his newspaper. "Jamie, what's with all the questions? You sound like your mother this morning."

"And what's that supposed to mean?" her mother asked angrily. "I suppose I do ask a lot of questions. At least I take an interest in what goes on around here. I don't hide behind a newspaper all morning."

Her father replied angrily without lowering the newspaper. Jamie turned her back on her bickering parents and tore the wrapping off the little package. Beneath the red wrapping paper was a black box.

She lifted open the lid of the box. Inside were two gold loop earrings.

Gold earrings?

"Oh, look! Earrings! How sweet!" her mother declared. She walked over and took them from Jamie's hand.

"Mother—"

"They're beautiful. Tom really has good taste." She held them up and examined them carefully. "Real gold. How did Tom ever afford these?"

"Shirl, give the girl a break. That's not a polite question," her father said.

But she's right, Jamie thought gloomily.

How did he afford them?

How could Tom ever afford to buy gold earrings?

He stole them, that's how!

He stole them from the Diamond Ranch, after he shot the manager.

And why did he bring them over early this morning and leave them for her?

There could only be one answer.

They were a threat.

They were meant to frighten her.

"You saw how I got these earrings," Tom was saying. "You saw the crime I committed. And now I have no choice but to kill you. . . ."

8

Jamie tossed the earrings onto the counter. "They're not really my taste," she said sadly.

But her parents weren't listening to her. They were off on another silly, trivial argument. They enjoyed this kind of mindless bickering. They did it all the time, about anything, about everything.

Their voices faded into the background as Jamie escaped into her own thoughts. Should she tell them the real reason Tom had brought the earrings? Should she tell them about the threatening phone call last night? Should she tell them what *really* happened at the dance?

No. They'd only start arguing about it.

They'd turn it into their own argument, and Jamie would lose control of the situation completely.

Control?

She smiled to herself. Her life was entirely out of control. How could she even think of that word?

"Jamie, how about some eggs this morning? Give you strength."

"No, Mom. I'm—" Then she gasped out loud as she saw the front-page headline on the newspaper section in her father's hands:

MALL JEWELER KILLED IN HOLDUP

"I'll scramble 'em real dry for you. They won't run all over the plate. I promise."

Jamie thought she might scream. How could her mother be talking about eggs?

So the jeweler had really died. Tom had killed him.

Tom was a murderer.

She grabbed the paper from her father's hands.

"Hey!" he cried, more surprised than angry. "What's the big idea? The Cloverhill score is in the sports section."

She didn't hear him. The words in the news article came at her in a jumble. She had to read the first sentence four times before it began to make sense to her.

Her eyes raced across the newspaper column. She couldn't concentrate enough to get the whole story. But she didn't need the whole story. The bits and pieces she was able to read were enough. . . .

"A young man with light blond hair was seen running through the parking lot. . . .

"The murder weapon was not found. . . .

"Police believe there were no witnesses to the crime. . . ."

Oh yes, there was, Jamie thought.

There was one witness. Me.

Of all people.

"Jamie, please, I wasn't finished with that section," her father insisted, reaching for the paper.

She slowly handed it back without looking at him.

"Since when are you so interested in the news?" he asked suspiciously.

"Oh. Uh . . . well . . ." She was thinking fast. "I have a Current Events test tomorrow. I just wanted to be ready for it."

For some reason, that ridiculous answer seemed to satisfy him. He shuffled through the paper, trying to find his place.

"Do you want two eggs or three?" her mother asked, opening the refrigerator door.

"Mom, really! I—"

A car horn honked in the driveway.

Jamie's mother jumped at the sound. "Who can that be?"

"Oh, I almost forgot," Jamie said, running to the front window. "It's Ann-Marie. We're going swimming at the Y this morning."

"Swimming? But what about your eggs? Jamie, you haven't had any breakfast at all!"

Jamie grabbed the half-eaten English muffin off her father's plate. "I'll just have this," she said.

The car horn honked again, longer this time.

Grateful to be getting out of the house, Jamie

stuffed the dry English muffin into her mouth and ran to get her swim bag.

Jamie adjusted her black, one-piece bathing suit and then plunged into the deep end. She quickly swam the length of the pool underwater and came up beside Ann-Marie, who was standing in the shallow end.

"Why do they keep this pool so warm?" Jamie asked, wiping water from her eyes with one hand and holding onto the pool wall with the other. "Yuck. It's like swimming in soup!"

Ann-Marie was struggling to push her red curls into the tight, rubber bathing cap the Y forced them to wear. She shivered. The air in the indoor pool area was so much colder than the water.

"It's for the germs," Ann-Marie said, concentrating on the bathing cap. "Germs and bacteria can't grow in cold water. So they keep the water as hot as they can."

"Oh. That explains it," Jamie said. She laughed. "Have you always been this twisted?"

"Only since I met you."

"I'm going to swim some laps," Jamie said, tired of waiting for Ann-Marie to get her hair tucked in. "I love having the whole pool to ourselves." She kicked off from the poolside, swimming in slow, steady strokes toward the deep end.

Ann-Marie looked around. "Hey, you're right! There's nobody else here!" She ripped the bathing cap from her head, tossed it out of the pool, and swam off toward Jamie.

They swam a few slow laps, then floated for a while, catching their breath. Jamie turned and floated on her back, pulling herself slowly toward the shallow end. Even in the annoyingly hot water, it felt good to be floating, to be weightless, to feel as if she were in a different, lighter world.

Moving lazily, feeling warm and comfortable, she gazed up past the balcony that overlooked the pool area to the dusty skylight above the pool. The skylight hadn't been cleaned in years. But somehow the sun managed to shine down, making the orange tiles of the pool shimmer like gold under the water.

It was so warm, so peaceful, so bright, she could almost forget her dark, heavy thoughts. Almost.

But when she plunged under the water and swam, pulling herself with long, even strokes, Tom's face followed her. And when she surfaced at the other end of the pool, gasping for breath, he was there, too.

She couldn't swim away from what had happened.

She couldn't swim away from her horror.

"Do you want to talk about last night?" Ann-Marie spoke softly, but her voice startled Jamie.

"Oh!"

"I'm sorry. I didn't mean to scare you."

They were both dog-paddling, moving their arms slowly and rhythmically in front of them.

"No. You didn't. I—uh—I'm still kinda jumpy," Jamie said. The understatement of the century!

"Is there anything I can do?" Ann-Marie asked.

"No. I don't know. I'm just having such a hard time deciding what to do," Jamie admitted. "I guess I've relied on Tom for so long, it's hard for me to make a decision by myself."

"Did he call you after—after the dance?" Ann-Marie asked, paddling to the side and grabbing hold of the edge.

"No. Well, yes." Jamie told her about the frightening phone call, and about being followed home, and about the gold earrings.

"Jamie, this is really scary. I think you should go to the police."

"I know," Jamie said reluctantly. "But once I do that, I'll never get to talk to Tom. I'll never hear his side of it. I'll never know what drove him to—what he was thinking when he—"

She looked away. She couldn't finish. She felt about to cry. But she didn't want to. She wasn't the kind of girl who cried. Even when she was little and would fall down and cut her knee, she'd force herself to hold the tears back.

What was the point of crying, anyway?

"Then you've just got to confront him," Ann-Marie said. Her voice sounded deep and echoey over the water. "But you've got to do it calmly this time."

Calmly.

Get serious.

Jamie believed she'd never feel calm again.

"You're right," she said, her voice a whisper. "I've got to talk to Tom first. I can't just go to the police and turn him in."

"Yeah. I think you should—" Ann-Marie was staring at the clock on the balcony wall. "Oh no! I forgot! I was supposed to call my aunt half an hour ago! I'm supposed to baby-sit for her some time today. Be right back."

She grabbed the ladder and pulled herself up. Her bare feet slapped loudly on the tiles as she hurried to the locker room to make her phone call.

Then the pool was silent, except for the whirr of the two ceiling fans and the splash of the water against the sides. Jamie swam a few laps, thinking about Tom, wondering how she could confront him calmly.

As she swam, she imagined their whole conversation. She imagined revealing to him that she was there in the jewelry store, hiding behind the counter, that she had seen everything, that she knew everything. He looked surprised at first, then very confused.

"But Jamie," she imagined him saying, "I wasn't at the mall yesterday afternoon. You must have seen someone else shoot that poor man. It wasn't me."

He looked so upset, so confused and hurt by her accusation that she knew he was telling the truth.

"Tom," she said, "I'm sorry. I'm so, so sorry. I'll never doubt you again."

Jamie smiled. It was all so simple. Confronting Tom was so easy—when she made up both sides of the conversation. And it all had such a happy ending.

Her arms felt tired and she had a slight cramp in her side. She turned onto her back and floated until the cramp began to ease. Back to the real world. Back to the world where she couldn't control both sides of the conversation. Where there was no happy ending.

What was keeping Ann-Marie?

Suddenly a shadow appeared across the middle of the pool.

She looked up to the skylight. No clouds had appeared to block the sun.

What was causing it?

She stood and stared into the blue waters. The narrow shadow floated a few yards away from her. It looked like the shadow of a large fish, or of a human.

Startled, she looked under the water. But she quickly realized that no creature could cast a shadow *up* toward the sunlight.

She looked back up to the skylight, and caught a glimpse of somebody peering down at her from the balcony above the pool. It was a young man. He pulled his head back as she looked up. But she saw blond hair, a frowning face.

Blond hair?

"Tom?" Jamie called. "Is that you?"

No reply.

The shadow had disappeared from the water.

She thought she heard scraping footsteps up on the balcony.

"Tom? Are you up there?" She was unable to keep the fear from her voice. She had to strain to call loudly enough to be heard. "Who's up there? Come on, is that you?"

Silence.

But she knew someone was up there. Someone had been watching her. She had seen him.

Suddenly feeling very frightened, she began to swim toward the steps at the shallow end. As she swam, she turned back looking for someone—anyone—who could help her. But the pool area was still empty.

Terror slowed her strokes, made her arms feel as if they each weighed a ton. She gasped for breath. Her heart pounded. She felt so alone, so vulnerable there in the middle of the silent, empty pool.

Finally she reached the steps and pulled herself up. She turned and looked up to the balcony. "Who is up there?" she called.

She stood on the steps, shivering, waiting, listening.

There was no reply.

Then from the balcony she heard the unmistakable sound of laughter, laughter soft but menacing.

9

I don't believe it. My aunt wants me over there in ten minutes. I just don't get a break. I—" Ann-Marie stopped as she saw Jamie's frightened face. "Jamie, what on earth!"

Jamie was running frantically across the wet tiles, her mouth open in a wide O of terror.

She pushed Ann-Marie back toward the locker room. "Let's get out of here! There's somebody up there!" She pushed open the locker room and, slipping on the wet floor, ran inside.

"Who? What do you mean?" Ann-Marie asked.

Jamie threw open her locker. She pulled off the wet bathing suit with frantic, fumbling hands, and, still dripping wet, began to pull on her clothes. "I mean there was someone up on the balcony spying on me. A guy."

"Are you sure?"

Jamie glared at her friend. "I'm not crazy, Ann-Marie." She struggled to pull her jeans over her wet legs. "You think I'm crazy, don't you! You think I'm cracking up!"

Why was she attacking Ann-Marie?

Maybe she really was cracking up.

"No. No, I don't," Ann-Marie said patiently. "I think you're very upset. You've been through a lot. You have every reason to be frightened and on edge."

"Thanks for your permission," Jamie snapped. She immediately regretted it. "Sorry."

Ann-Marie shrugged. She rolled up her bathing suit and pushed it into a white plastic bag. She tossed her towel into the narrow, gray locker and started to get dressed.

"There was someone up on the balcony," Jamie continued, her hands shaking as she pulled on her sweatshirt. "When I looked up, he ducked back so I couldn't see him. I thought I saw blond hair. I thought it was Tom. But when I called up to him . . . when I called his name . . . he didn't answer. I just heard laughing. It wasn't Tom's regular laugh at all. It was . . . evil. Like he was trying to scare me."

Ann-Marie sat down on the low wooden bench to tie her sneakers. "How gross," she said, shaking her head.

"But why would Tom do that to me?" Jamie asked, sounding more bewildered than frightened. "Why wouldn't he want to face me, to talk?"

"Maybe it wasn't him," Ann-Marie said. "You know, lots of times boys sneak over from the boys' pool and hide out on the balcony to spy on girls. It was probably just some kid."

"Well, maybe." Jamie wanted to believe Ann-Marie. But something told her that it wasn't a kid playing a prank up on the balcony. She shook her wet hair and then pushed it behind her shoulder.

"That would explain the evil laughing," Ann-Marie continued. "It was just some dumb kid."

"And I'm a total paranoid," Jamie said, forcing a smile.

"I didn't say that!" Ann-Marie cried defensively. She grabbed Jamie by the shoulders. "You're terribly upset. I understand. It's a nightmare, a horrible nightmare. And it won't end until . . . until . . ."

"Until what?" Jamie asked, about to burst into tears despite all of her efforts to hold them back.

"Until you talk to Tom," Ann-Marie said, letting go and turning to pick up her swim bag. "Until you hear what happened from his lips. Until you know the truth."

"But I already know the truth!" Jamie insisted, hating the hysterical sound in her voice. "I don't want to know the truth! That's the whole problem, isn't it? The truth is the problem! What happened yesterday afternoon is the problem. What Tom did in that jewelry store is the problem. Don't you see, Ann-Marie? I don't want the truth to be the truth!"

Ann-Marie lightly put an arm around Jamie's shoulders. Jamie shivered. Her shoulders shook as if she were about to cry. But instead, she pulled away from her friend and grabbed up her swimming bag.

"I'm going right over to Tom's house," she said. "I'm going to confront him. I'm going to hear the truth. I've got to know." She slammed her locker shut.

Two girls, both blond and very skinny, came into the locker room. They were giggling about something. One of them gave the other a playful shove and they began giggling again.

Jamie watched them with envy.

She wondered if she'd ever laugh again over something trivial and silly.

The two girls looked as if they didn't have a care in the world. They noticed her staring at them. She quickly looked away. They giggled again.

"My aunt's house is in Beresford, the other direction," Ann-Marie said, holding the locker room door for Jamie. "But I guess I could drop you at Tom's. I'd only be a little bit late."

"No. Don't be silly," Jamie insisted. The air in the main hallway of the Y was hot and steamy. The desk clerk sat in a folding chair, his chin on his chest, snoring loudly. "I don't want to make you late. The bus stop is just two blocks from here."

"Are you sure you don't mind? You'll be okay?"

Jamie shrugged. "I'll be okay," she said, frowning.

I'll never be okay again, she thought.

They pushed open the front door and stepped out into the white glare of midday sunshine. "Wow!" They both shielded their eyes from the unexpected brightness.

"What a gorgeous day!" Ann-Marie exclaimed.

"I can't see a thing!" Jamie said, searching her bag for her sunglasses. Of course, she had forgotten to bring them.

Ann-Marie hurried down the steps and headed toward her car. "I'll call you from my aunt's," she shouted. "If you're not home yet, I'll leave my aunt's phone number with your folks."

"Okay," Jamie called after her. But her voice came out a whisper. She suddenly felt very weak and tired. The overwhelming sun made her feel even more helpless.

Was she really going to Tom's?

Was she really going to sit down in Tom's den and say, "Guess what? I saw you shoot that little man in the jewelry store yesterday afternoon."

Couldn't she just disappear instead?

Couldn't she just melt away under this hot sun? Couldn't she just fade, fade away until she was only an invisible sunbeam, a white glare on the pavement?

No.

She had no choice.

She turned and, still feeling weak, started toward the bus stop. She had to force her legs to carry her there. They didn't seem to want to move at all. It was almost as if they were pulling her back.

"Look out!"

A boy came roaring past her on a BMX bike that looked much too big for him.

She jumped out of the way. But the boy had already swerved past her. He turned his head and grinned back at her. Then he raced around the corner and disappeared.

Her heart pounding, Jamie forced herself to walk faster. She felt as if she were moving in slow motion. What was wrong with her? She hadn't jumped out of the way of the bike until it was well past her.

She crossed the street, remembering to look for oncoming cars only when she was halfway across. She squinted against the white sunlight and continued walking.

A squirrel, standing at the base of a tree trunk with its head toward the ground and its tail straight up in the air, stared at her as she walked by. As she drew near, it turned and started to dash up the tree trunk, then hesitated, started again, leaped off the tree and ran across the wide green yard behind it.

"I know how you feel," Jamie said aloud. She wanted to run away, too.

She heard a footstep on the sidewalk behind her.

She turned quickly.

There was no one there.

She picked up her pace. The bus stop was just a block away. She looked down the street to see if the bus was coming. No. It didn't run very often on Sundays. But maybe she'd get lucky and not have to wait in the sun too long.

Another footstep.

She turned.

Yes. Someone was there. She saw a shadow slip behind the tree the squirrel had occupied.

"Tom, is that you?"

Don't be ridiculous. Why would it be Tom?

She started to jog.

The fear was back. The fear was weighing her down again.

But she knew she couldn't let it.

She had to run. She forced herself to run.

She stumbled over a rock on the walk, but kept going. She looked back as she ran. The shadow slipped out from behind the tree. It was moving along the tall evergreen bushes that lined the sidewalk.

She forced her legs forward. She was running as fast as she could now.

She saw the orange and black bus turn the corner.

Half a block to go.

Footsteps behind her. Getting closer. Closer.

Who was chasing her?

She couldn't turn around, couldn't stop.

There was no one else at the bus shelter. No one to see her. No one to help her.

She waved to the bus driver, a desperate signal to help her, to stop the bus, to stop her pursuer.

The bus rumbled past.

She wasn't sure the driver had seen her.

Would the bus stop?

The footsteps were right behind her.

She could hear heavy breathing, a gasp with each pound of foot against sidewalk.

The sun made everything go white, whiter than white.

She reached the deserted bus shelter. She waved desperately to the driver.

The bus stopped.

The doors slowly swung open.

She started up the first step onto the bus.

And two powerful hands grabbed her around the waist.

10

Jamie tried to scream. But no sound came out.

Using strength she didn't know she had, the desperate strength that comes to those in their moment of deepest trouble, she pulled away from the hands that held her.

She leaped onto the bus and grabbed hold of the change box to support herself. The doors closed behind her.

"Did you see him?" she cried to the driver, her voice high and wild, an animal shriek.

The driver had his head out the window. She saw that he was adjusting his rearview mirror.

"Please, did you see him?" Jamie repeated, still gripping the money box.

The driver slowly pulled his head in and turned to her. "You need a transfer?" He was a big man, almost too fat to fit behind the wheel. His uniform shirt was open, the narrow red tie pulled loose. He badly needed a shave.

She looked down the long bus. It was empty. She was the only passenger.

Humming to himself, the driver turned the big wheel and stepped on the gas. The bus lurched forward. Jamie stumbled into the first seat.

She looked out the window at the bus shelter. There was no one there.

No one on the sidewalk. No one in the street.

They passed the boy on his BMX bike. The boy waved to the driver. The driver ignored him.

"Did you see someone behind me?" Jamie asked, sitting down and searching the swim bag for her change purse.

"Sorry, miss. I can't wait for your friend," the driver said, misunderstanding. "I've got a schedule to keep. Even on Sunday, believe it or not."

"No. No. There was someone there. I mean, someone was behind me. He—"

"Sorry." He turned the wheel hard to avoid a pothole in the street, almost throwing Jamie from the seat. "I wasn't looking. I've been trying to get that mirror right all morning. You know how it is when it's off just a little bit and you can't get it the way you want it? It's a little thing, but it drives me bananas. Know what I mean? Do you drive? Oh. You're too young, huh?"

"I have my temporary permit," Jamie said.

She found the right change, stood up, and dropped

it into the box. "You okay?" the driver asked, glancing away from the road to look at her.

"I—I'm okay." Jamie didn't want to talk anymore. She thought of walking to the back of the bus to get away from him. But she didn't want to appear rude.

"I've got a daughter," the driver said, making a wide turn onto Maplewood Drive. "But she ain't like you. She's a big girl. Too big. I guess she takes after her dad. Ha ha!"

Jamie didn't know what to say. She stared out the window. She tried to stop from shaking. But she could still feel the strong hands around her waist. She could still feel them grasping her as she struggled to climb onto the bus.

Who had it been?

And how had he disappeared so quickly?

"I don't know why I buy them for her. I guess it's hard to say no. Know what I mean?" the driver was saying, gesturing with both hands, letting the wheel guide itself.

Jamie had no idea what he was talking about. "Yeah. I guess," she said.

They were just a few blocks from Tom's house. If only she could stop trembling . . .

She wanted Tom to comfort her, to put his arms around her the way he always did when she was nervous or upset, to pull her close and make her feel warm and safe.

Warm and safe.

She uttered a loud sigh.

She would never be able to feel warm and safe with Tom again.

With anyone, maybe.

She had trusted him. She had loved him. She had built her life around him.

And he was a murderer.

"Well, she didn't exactly mean it that way. But that's how it came out," the driver was saying.

They passed Creedmore and Van Buren, passed houses Jamie knew so well. She had been coming to this neighborhood for so many years. Such a happy place. Such a pretty place.

"I'm not that strict, but I believe in discipline. Know what I mean? I'm a pretty understanding guy, but sometimes . . ."

"The next stop is mine," Jamie said quietly.

She suddenly felt cold all over.

She ran her hands back over her long, black hair. It was still wet. Feeling the tangles, she realized she hadn't remembered to brush it back at the Y. She probably looked like a wild woman. No wonder the bus driver had asked her if she was okay.

He stopped the bus at the corner on Sherwood. She forced herself to stand up, and started down the steps. "Thanks," she called back to him.

"Nice talking to you," he said cheerfully. "Have a nice day."

The doors closed behind her. She stood motionless on the corner as the empty bus rumbled away.

Have a nice day?

Did he say to have a nice day?

The sun poured down, hotter than before, but it didn't warm her. She took a deep breath and looked up the block toward Tom's house. No car in the drive. The front door was closed. Maybe no one was home.

Then what would she do?

Run away? Wait? Go crazy?

She forced herself to stop thinking, to walk and not think. She tried to make her mind as blank and white as the sunlight.

But it was impossible.

How many times had she made this short walk from the corner to Tom's house? How many times had she passed the sprawling red brick ranch house on the corner, then the white frame house with the black shuttered windows, and walked up the gravel drive to the small front stoop surrounded by pansies and geraniums? And knocked on the screen door? And waited eagerly to be invited into the little house?

Sure, it was much smaller than the other houses on the block. And sure, it was badly in need of painting. And the gutters were in disrepair. And the shingles had fallen off one side of the small garage.

But it was such a warm place.

It had always meant so much warmth to Jamie, such warm feelings, such feelings of love.

She stepped over the Sunday paper, pulled open the screen door, and, remembering that the doorbell was broken, knocked on the door.

Was this the last time she'd be knocking on this door? The last time she'd be standing on this stoop?

All that warmth, all that love, lost forever.

She peered into the small window in the door. The house was dark. No one was coming to answer her knock.

She knocked again.

And waited.

One more try.

She turned to leave.

The door was suddenly pulled open.

Startled, she spun around and started to say hi. But she stopped with her mouth open.

The man at the door was a total stranger.

"I—I'm sorry. I must have the wrong house," Jamie said. She started to back away and tripped over the Sunday newspaper.

She caught herself in the gutter downspout, and pulled herself up. "Sorry." She felt like a complete idiot.

She looked up at the house, trying to figure out her mistake, and realized it was the right house after all.

The young man at the door stared at her, looking a little startled. He appeared to be in his mid-twenties, but he was already going bald. He was very sunburned, and his forehead was almost lobster red. Despite the heat, he was wearing a dark sports jacket and a tie.

"Are you Jamie?" he asked.

"Yes. How did you—"

"I'm Eric Goodwyn." He reached out a sunburned hand to shake hers. "I work with Tom's dad."

She had to let go of the downspout to reach his hand. She'd never felt so awkward, so horribly uncomfortable and embarrassed in all her life. "I'm Jamie," she said. "Oh. You already knew that."

He pushed open the screen door for her to come in. She reluctantly stepped forward, being careful not to trip over the rubber welcome mat.

The living room was dark and cool. She couldn't see anything at all for a few seconds. It took her eyes a long time to adjust from the bright sunlight.

"I—I was looking for Tom," she said. Her voice caught. She sounded so nervous.

But what could she do? She *was* nervous.

Where was Tom? Where was his mom? Why was this man here all alone?

"Do you want to sit down?" Eric gestured to the couch. He stood stiffly behind an armchair. He seemed awkward and uncomfortable too.

"Thanks." She dropped her swim bag to the floor and sat down on the couch.

"I'm afraid I have some bad news," Eric said, his upper lip twitching. He scratched at his sunburned bald head.

Oh no, Jamie thought. Tom has been arrested. The police have arrested him for the murder of the jeweler. Of course. That's where everyone is!

She couldn't say anything. She stared up at Eric, feeling cold and shivery, and waited for him to tell her what she already knew.

"Tom's dad was in a bad auto accident upstate," Eric said, gripping the back of the armchair.

"What?" Jamie cried in surprise.

She realized immediately that it was an inappropriate reaction. "Oh, how horrible!" she added quickly.

"Tom and his mom got the call early this morning, at about nine-thirty, I guess," Eric said, drumming his red fingers on the back of the chair.

"I'm so sorry," she said quietly, looking past Eric to the hallway.

"I was here when they got the call. I'd come over to pick up some papers. They rushed upstate immediately," Eric continued. "They left in a terrible hurry, as you can imagine. I stayed to get the cat and close up the house for them."

"I see." She couldn't think of anything else to say.

"Are you okay?" he asked suddenly. "Can I get you a drink of water or something?"

"No. I mean yes. I'll get it." She jumped up and started for the kitchen. "Is Tom's dad—is he—?"

"We don't know," Eric said, following her. He shrugged. "The person who called from the hospital said he was in critical condition. That doesn't sound good."

"No. I guess not," Jamie said quietly.

If Tom had rushed upstate at nine-thirty, he couldn't have been the one spying on me from the balcony at the Y, she thought.

She pulled a glass down from the cabinet and went to the refrigerator for the water pitcher. "Want some?" she asked Eric. "You look awfully hot."

"No. No thanks," he said. He loosened his tie.

And if Tom was upstate, it couldn't have been him who chased me to the bus stop, she thought.

So who was it?

She drank too fast, nearly choked, spilled water on her sweatshirt. Eric pretended not to notice.

She put the empty glass down on the counter. "I—uh—guess I'd better be going," she said.

She suddenly wanted to get out of there, get away from Tom's house, from all of the familiar things in it. She had to think, to figure out what was happening to her, what she should do next.

"I'll—uh—I'll call later. Do you think they'll be back?" she asked.

Eric scratched his red forehead. It seemed to be a habit he had. Maybe he was checking to see if any hair had grown back. "Hard to say," he told her. "But you can try."

"Well, thanks. I mean, not for the bad news. For telling me." She started back toward the living room to get her bag.

"Oh, wait!" he came running after her. "I almost forgot. I guess I'm a little scattered. Here. Tom left this for you."

He handed her a small white envelope.

"Thanks," she said. Her heart began to pound. She took the envelope. She felt her chest tighten. It was hard to breathe.

What was in the envelope? A confession? An admission of his guilt? An admission that he had seen her there in the jewelry store?

Was it an apology? An apology for betraying their future? For ruining their lives forever? Or was it another threat, like the gold earrings?

"You can stay and read it," Eric offered. "I'm just going to turn off the lights upstairs and then lock up."

"No. No, that's okay. It was nice meeting you. I mean, I'm sorry we had to meet this way. Oh, you know what I mean."

Gripping the small envelope tightly in her hand, she took her swim bag and hurried out the front door. The screen door slammed behind her. She stepped off the front stoop into the white glare of the midafternoon sun, and ran blindly down the gravel driveway.

Dear Jamie,

It wasn't me in the jewelry store yesterday afternoon. It must have been someone else. I hope you like the earrings. They were my grandmother's.

I don't want you to worry about anything. I will be back as soon as we know how my dad is doing, and then everything will go back to the way it was before.

I am sorry for the rough time you've been through. But it's all a big misunderstanding. Please believe me when I say that everything will be fine.

Love,
Tom

That's what Jamie imagined the note would say. That's what Jamie *prayed* the note would say.

She tossed the swim bag over her shoulder and began to run toward the bus stop. She held the envelope tightly, staring at it, repeating in her mind what she wanted it to say. The bright sun made the white envelope glow. It felt hot in her palm.

I have to read it—now—before it burns a hole in my hand, she thought.

She scolded herself for such crazy thoughts.

Once again, she ran over in her mind what she wanted it to say.

Out of breath, she stopped in front of the red brick ranch house on the corner. There didn't seem to be anyone home. She dropped to the grass. She started to tear open the envelope.

Before she could get it open, something jumped on her, yapping, scratching, hopping onto her lap. It was the little brown-and-white fox terrier from across the street.

"Down, Rudy! Get down!" she cried.

Rudy yipped playfully and tried to pull the envelope from her hand with his teeth.

"No! Bad dog! Bad dog! Rudy, go home!"

She jerked the envelope away and tried to climb to her feet. But the little dog was fast, and determined. Rudy pulled the envelope out of her hand and started to run back across the street with it.

"No!" she screamed. She dived after the little dog, missed, scrambled to her feet and dived again.

Keeping the envelope tightly between its teeth, the dog dodged away from her. Its stub of a tail was vibrating with excitement. It was obviously enjoying this game a great deal.

I don't believe this, Jamie thought. *This stupid dog*

is running away with the most important note of my life!

She moved slowly, stealthily toward the animal. "Rudy, drop. Drop. Good dog."

The dog backed away, out of her reach.

I'm smarter than this dog, Jamie thought. I've got to think of a way to outsmart it.

She looked for a stick to throw. Perhaps the dog would drop the envelope to go after the stick. But there were no sticks. The people who lived in the red-brick ranch house kept their lawn spotless. There wasn't even a leaf on it.

"Rudy, drop."

The stupid dog didn't understand English!

Then she had an idea. Quickly she pulled her bag off her shoulder and unzipped it. "Here, Rudy, look. Look what's inside!" She dropped the bag to the ground and held it open.

It worked.

The curious dog dropped the envelope and ran to stick its snout into the open swim bag.

Jamie snatched the envelope off the grass. The dog was busy pulling her wet swimsuit out of the bag, but she ignored it. She tore open the envelope, which was wet and sticky from Rudy's mouth, and pulled out the note.

She unfolded it, her hands shaking. At her feet, the dog growled and snapped, flinging the wet bathing suit around. Then it went back to the bag to pull out her bath towel.

The note had been scrawled in pencil, obviously written in great haste, for Tom usually had very neat and precise handwriting. It was shorter than the one she had imagined, and a lot less satisfying:

Dear Jamie—

I guess we all act crazy sometimes. I'll try to call you.

Love,
Tom

The dog growled and snapped the wet towel at Jamie's ankles.

"Ouch! Dumb dog! Go home!"

What did the note mean?

We all act crazy?

Was Tom admitting that he had acted crazy by holding up the jewelry store and killing the owner?

Or was the note referring to how crazy Jamie had acted at the dance the night before?

She read the note again and again until the words all became meaningless.

We all act crazy?

The dog slapped her again with the wet towel. But when she continued to ignore him, he got bored with the game. He poked around in her bag, saw that it was now empty, and quickly trotted back across the street, carrying Jamie's towel in his teeth.

Jamie sat down on the grass. She felt more bewildered than before. She had only questions now. No answers. No clues.

What did Tom's note mean? Was it an apology, or an accusation?

If Tom was upstate, who had chased her this morning?

And who had chased her after the dance last night?

Was it possible that she imagined both incidents?

She had imagined stabbing Tom in the workroom. Couldn't she also have imagined being chased by some mysterious pursuer?

And then she thought of the most horrifying questions of all: What if she also imagined the holdup? What if she only imagined that it was Tom in the jewelry store? What if she really was cracking up?

12

I'm sorry, Casey. *Zoomey* is not a word."

"Of course it is," Casey insisted, refusing to pick up the letters from the board.

"Don't be stupid," Jamie said.

"Don't call your brother stupid," Jamie's mother said from across the room.

"Casey, I'm not going to play Scrabble with you if you insist on making words like *zoomey,"* Jamie said, not meaning to sound as angry as she did.

"But zoomey is a word," Casey whined. "Don't you ever feel zoomey?"

"Aaaaagggh!"

"Jamie, don't scream at your brother. Why can't you two ever play a game without screaming at each other?" Jamie's mother was watching an old movie on TV and listening to the Scrabble game at the same time.

"I'm going to bed," Jamie's dad said. "I like to turn

in early on Sunday night. It gives me a good head start for the week." He started toward the stairs.

"Head start for what?" Jamie's mom had to comment on every word that was said, whether it required comment or not. "Are you in a race?"

Her father ignored the question and continued up the stairs.

"Why do you have to pick on Dad?" Jamie asked irritably.

"Because I get tired of picking on you," her mother cracked.

"No, you don't. You never get tired of picking on me," Jamie said.

Why was she doing this? Why was she starting a fight with her mother for no reason at all?

"Okay, okay," Casey said. He pulled up the letters and slammed some new ones onto the board with his stubby fingers.

"Zoomoid?" Jamie cried. "Are you crazy?"

"Don't call your brother crazy," came the remark from across the room.

"Leave us alone and let us play!" Jamie screamed, feeling herself lose control but not able to do anything about it.

"Don't scream at me, young lady." Her mother started switching from channel to channel with her remote control unit.

"Don't call me young lady!" Jamie shouted. "I hate when you call me young lady! It sounds like something from a bad TV sitcom!"

"Okay, okay," Casey said, holding his hands over

his ears to block out the shrill voices. "I'll change the word. I'll just make it *zoom.*"

"Just calm down," her mother said. "Don't get hysterical."

"I'm not hysterical!" Jamie shrieked.

"How about *zoomer?*" Casey suggested, plunking an *E* and *R* down on the board. "You know, the plane is a real zoomer."

"I quit! I've had it!" Jamie tilted the board, spilling all of the letters onto the table, pushed back her chair and ran up to her room.

"What's the matter with *her?*" she heard Casey ask.

"She's upset because Tom's father was in a car accident," her mom explained.

She should only know why I'm upset! Jamie thought.

"But why'd she have to wreck the game?" Casey asked disgustedly.

Jamie slammed the door to her room.

She was furious at herself for behaving like such an idiot. And now she'd have to spend all of breakfast apologizing to Casey for spoiling the game, and to her mother for throwing a fit.

"Aaaaggggh!"

She picked her chemistry notebook off the desk and heaved it at the wall. Its spine hit with a loud *thud,* and all of the pages flew out and scattered over the floor.

"Oh great," she said sarcastically. "Good move, ace."

She didn't bother to pick them up. She stepped over them and grabbed her phone. She punched Tom's number for the three thousandth time that evening.

She let it ring at least a dozen times, then slammed the receiver down so hard the whole phone fell off the desk. It clattered to the floor at her feet. She kicked at it angrily, then scooped it up and put it back in its place.

Kicking chemistry papers out of her way, she threw herself onto the bed. "I'm out of control, out of control, out of control," she repeated aloud, banging her fists against the pink and white quilted bedspread.

She realized that acting crazy wasn't making her feel any better. In fact, it was making her feel much worse.

She had always been a very controlled person. The reason she almost never cried was that she believed in acting reasonably, logically, not emotionally.

Sometimes she had made fun of Tom because he was much more emotional than she. At the movies, he was always the one with tears in his eyes at the sad parts. And when they had arguments, he was always the one to get hysterical first and lose the whole thread of what they were arguing about. She won a lot of arguments by staying cool and thinking clearly.

Only in her feelings for Tom, she realized, did her calm levelheadedness abandon her. Her feelings for Tom went beyond emotion. At times, she felt as if she might burst from loving him so much.

She couldn't live without him.

But now she was going to have to.

"No! It isn't fair!" The desperate, shrill sound of her voice frightened her.

"Stop it, Jamie," she told herself. "Stop it right now."

She turned onto her back and stared up at the cracks in the ceiling. She froze there, taking slow, deep breaths, waiting to feel calm, waiting for the feeling of sheer panic to drain away.

She stared up at the cracks, trying to see the animals she used to find up there when she was a little girl. She remembered that the cracks formed an astounding menagerie.

Why couldn't she see any animals now?

Why did the cracks just look like cracks to her?

"Where did the animals go?" she asked aloud.

Annoyed, still feeling strange and panicky, she jumped up and went back to the phone. "Tom, why aren't you home? I've got to try your number one more time."

She reached for the receiver.

And the phone rang.

It startled her. She dropped the receiver, fumbled with the cord, finally retrieved it.

"Hello?"

"Hello, darling. This is Aunt Sarah. How are you, darling?"

Jamie's least favorite aunt. The most long-winded person in the world.

She's going to stay on the phone for two hours, and Tom won't be able to reach me, Jamie thought.

"Fine, Aunt Sarah," she said through gritted teeth.

"I haven't seen you for so long, honeybun. You're such a doll. I'll bet you're even more gorgeous than the last time I saw you."

How am I going to keep from screaming at this woman? Jamie asked herself. She realized she was gripping the receiver so tightly, her hand hurt.

"Thank you, Aunt Sarah."

"When *was* the last time I saw you?" her aunt continued. "Let me think." There was an endless pause.

"I don't remember, Aunt Sarah. But listen, I've really got to—"

"Was it at your cousin's wedding? When was that? December, right?"

"I don't know. I really—"

"No. I must've seen you since then. Let me think."

Jamie paced rapidly back and forth over the scattered chemistry papers. She had the phone cord between her teeth and felt as if she could bite right through it.

"Oh, I know. It was at Irma's housewarming party. Remember?"

"Yes, of course," Jamie said, unable to keep the impatience from her voice.

"That's quite a house Irma got. She's a lucky, lucky woman."

"Yes. Right."

I'm going to die here on the phone, Jamie thought. They're going to find me lying on the floor here in the morning, and Aunt Sarah will still be talking into my right ear.

"Well, it's been much too long," Aunt Sarah continued in her raspy, cigarette-roughened voice. "Much, much too long. Irma's party was when? January? No. February. Yes. Much too long, sweetie."

"Yes, you're right."

"Listen, Jamie, is Shirl still up? I want to talk to her for a minute."

A minute? That meant at least two hours!

"I'll go get her."

She put down the receiver and opened the door to her room. "Mom," she yelled downstairs. "Aunt Sarah's on the phone."

"Don't yell," her mother shouted back from the living room. "Your father's trying to sleep."

"Please don't talk long," Jamie pleaded, a little softer.

"What did you say? I can't hear you if you mumble. Never mind."

She heard her mother pick up the phone and begin to talk.

Please, please don't stay on all night, Jamie thought.

She slumped back to her room, suddenly feeling weary and drained. She could hear her aunt droning on about something as she replaced the receiver on her phone. Then she stooped down and started to collect the chemistry papers from the floor.

I'll never get them back in order, she thought.

I'll never get anything in my life back in order.

She sat down at the desk and tried to put the

notebook back together. A few minutes later, she picked up the phone. Aunt Sarah and her mother were still talking.

She replaced the receiver, then sat staring at Tom's picture for a long while. She liked the picture, even though his hair was so short in it. He had completely forgotten about class pictures and had gotten a haircut the day before.

He had the beginnings of a smile in the photo, as if he were enjoying some private joke. The tie they'd made him wear was too fat. And his shirt collar was torn. Jamie remembered how embarrassed he was about that.

Embarrassed enough to rob a jewelry store?

Embarrassed enough to shoot a man?

She turned the photo toward the wall.

She could feel the panic welling up inside her again. She picked up the phone. They were still talking.

She took a deep breath and opened her mouth to yell, "Get off the phone!" But she slammed the receiver down instead. Maybe they'd take the hint.

She decided she might as well get undressed and ready for bed. She pulled off her jeans and the sweatshirt she'd been wearing all day and tossed them onto the chair by the window.

She was just pulling on a nightgown when the phone rang again.

13

Hi, Jamie. It's me. Did Tom call?"

"Oh. Hi, Ann-Marie."

"You don't have to sound *that* disappointed, do you?"

"I'm sorry. I just—I thought you were Tom."

"I guess that means he hasn't called."

"No. I've tried his house about a million times. No answer. I guess they're not back from upstate. I don't know if that's good news or bad news—I mean, about his father."

"Are you okay? You sound really strange, sort of beyond tired."

"I'm okay, I guess. No. Actually, I'm a basket case. But what can I do?" Jamie nervously tangled the phone cord round and around her wrist.

"Do you want to talk?"

"No. I think I'd better leave the line clear. You

know. In case Tom tries to call." She glanced at her desk clock. Eleven-fifteen.

"Okay. Well, hang in. I'll come pick you up before school tomorrow morning."

"Okay. Thanks."

"Get some sleep."

"Sleep? Oh. Right. I'll try."

She replaced the receiver, stood up, and stretched. She'd forgotten about sleep. Sleep might not be a bad idea. It was certainly a good way to make time pass quickly. She turned off the lamp and climbed under the bedspread.

Of course, getting to sleep was not going to be easy. The room seemed to spin in the dark. She closed her eyes, but the feeling of dizziness didn't go away.

Stop thinking, she told herself.

Stop picturing Tom. Stop talking to Tom. Stop all of the imaginary conversations.

How could she blot out the pictures that flashed in her mind, slow her racing pulse, stop the dark room from twirling so recklessly?

She conjured up clouds. Soft, billowing white clouds in a clear blue sky. She followed the clouds as they drifted slowly to the right, trailed by new, fluffy clouds, drifting, drifting, drifting. . . .

A loud tapping sound made the clouds disappear.

She opened her eyes and sat up.

The tapping repeated. Two hard taps followed by three soft taps.

"Oh!"

Someone was crouched outside her window.

"Tom!"

She jumped from the bed, tripping over the bedspread, and ran to pull open the window. He smiled at her, a shadowy smile. The moonlight caught the front of his white-blond hair, illuminating his anxious face.

"Tom, what are you doing up here? When did you get back?"

He dropped easily into the room. His arms went around her. He pulled her close. He felt cold, his sweater felt cold, even though it was a warm spring night.

After a while, he let go. She turned on the lamp. His jeans were dirty, probably from climbing up to her room. His sweater was torn down the front.

"I had to see you, Jamie. I had to explain."

She took both of his hands and pulled him over to the bed. "Sit down, Tom. You look so tired. How is your dad?"

The question seemed to surprise him. He tossed a hand back through his white-blond hair, then shook his head. "I don't know," he said, looking back toward the window. He looked more troubled than Jamie had ever seen him. Troubled and exhausted.

"Will he be okay?" Jamie asked. "Is he still in critical condition?"

Tom looked confused. "I don't know," Tom whispered. "I don't want to talk about it."

"I've been so worried," Jamie said. She was still gripping both of his hands tightly. They were so cold. She wanted to warm them.

But he pulled his hands away suddenly and stood up. He walked over to the desk, then back to the window. "I want to explain," he said, balling his hands into fists, then unballing them and stuffing his hands into his jeans pockets.

He walked back to the desk, then took a few steps toward the bed. He was obviously very nervous. He looked as if he wanted to jump out of his body, to escape from it into thin air.

"What do you want to explain?" she asked softly, dreading what she was about to hear.

"You shouldn't have gone into that jewelry store," he said, his eyes glowing black in the dim lamplight. His whole face seemed to harden. "You shouldn't have seen what you saw in there."

"Ohh." Jamie uttered a loud sigh, a sigh of hopelessness, of complete resignation. "So it really was you?" Her voice was the tiniest whisper.

Until the last moment, until those last words, she had hoped against hope that it hadn't been him in the jewelry store. But now he had admitted it.

It was over.

All over.

She slumped back against the wall, feeling too weak to sit up.

"Yes, it was me," Tom said, moving closer, his eyes narrowed, staring coldly at her. "You saw me. You were there and you saw me. And now I have no choice."

"What do you mean?" A chill ran down her back, a tingle of fear.

"I have no choice. I have to kill you."

With a sudden motion, he picked up her pillow and pushed it over her face.

Using both hands, using all of her strength, she pushed the pillow away and stared up at him, her eyes pleading, her mouth twisted in terror.

"But why, Tom, why?"

"Because now you know my secret," he said flatly. His voice revealed no emotion at all. Neither did his blank, unmoving eyes.

"Your secret?"

"Yes. Now you know that there are two of me!"

He pressed the pillow forward again.

"Tom, wait! Let's talk! Let's—"

He pulled the pillow back and stood up straight. "You know my secret," he said, still revealing no emotion at all.

He snapped his fingers.

A second Tom, an identical Tom, suddenly stood beside the first Tom.

"You know my secret, too," the second Tom said, his voice identical to the first Tom.

Both Toms raised their pillows and moved forward in unison to smother her.

Jamie made no move to resist.

It was over.

All over.

There was nothing to fight for, no reason to resist.

She accepted the pillows almost gratefully as they pushed against her face, two identical pillows from two identical Toms, blocking out the light, blocking out the air. . . .

She awoke with a scream in her throat and her pillow resting on top of her face.

What a horrible nightmare!

She looked around the room. It was still night. The window was closed. There was no one there.

A nightmare. She was shaking all over.

What was that noise?

The phone was ringing.

How long had it been ringing?

Her heart pounding, her head throbbing, she climbed out of bed and picked up the receiver. "Tom?" she asked.

"Don't try to run away from me," the muffled voice at the other end said, menace in every word. "You can't get away."

"Tom? Is that you?"

"You shouldn't have seen me in the mall Saturday. Now you have to be punished."

14

Jamie, you've *got* to call the police!"

"I know. I know." Jamie yawned loudly, unable to fully wake up. She hadn't been able to fall back to sleep after the horrifying nightmare and the threatening phone call.

They walked past the Hofflers' house. Mrs. Hoffler was already out weeding around the patio. She stopped to wave a rubber-gloved hand as the two girls passed by her front yard.

"How come we're walking to school?" Jamie asked. "I thought you were going to pick me up in your car."

An exaggerated look of shock spread across Ann-Marie's freckled face. "My car? Oh, good lord! I forgot it!"

"Very funny," Jamie said, frowning. She didn't have the strength to laugh at Ann-Marie's jokes this morning.

"Sorry," Ann-Marie said, shifting her book bag onto her other shoulder. "My dad's car is in the garage. So he needed mine this morning. I was just trying to cheer you up."

"What's the point?" Jamie asked sullenly.

They walked on toward Cloverhill High in silence. The morning sun was pale, and the air was still cold. A bank of dark clouds rose to the west. Jamie noticed that the rows of red and yellow tulips in the Winklers' garden were already starting to droop and fall away. Spring was nearly over, but the weather didn't seem to realize it.

"We could go to the police if you don't want to call them," Ann-Marie suggested as they crossed Waverly and turned onto Welch. "I'd go with you."

"Yeah. Maybe we should," Jamie said, not really listening to Ann-Marie, listening instead to the threatening voice from the call the night before, repeating again and again in her head.

"I mean, this is serious," Ann-Marie said, stopping abruptly in the middle of the street as two fifth graders on bikes pedaled by. "You are an eyewitness to a crime. You can get into serious trouble for not reporting what you saw."

"How could I be in any more serious trouble?" Jamie moaned. "My life is ruined forever. That's enough serious trouble."

Ann-Marie could see there was little use trying to reason with Jamie. But she continued to try anyway. "You've been physically threatened. You've been chased. You've been grabbed. And the phone calls . . . Are you sure it was Tom?"

"Oh, I don't know," Jamie moaned. "It sounded like him, but it didn't. It sounded like him if he tried to disguise his voice. But in a way, it didn't. I'm just so confused, Ann-Marie. If only I could talk to him."

"Well, did you—"

"I called his house right after the threatening call. It rang and rang. There was no one there. They were still upstate, I guess."

"Did the threatening call sound like it was long distance?"

"I couldn't tell. No. I don't think so."

"Well, this is too scary to keep to yourself. I know you're not going to feel great about it, Jamie. But I really think you'll feel a little better, a little relieved at least, if you tell the story to the police."

Jamie thought about it as the two-story, yellow brick high school came into view. "Okay," she said finally. "I'll go after school. Will you really come with me?"

"Sure," Ann-Marie said. "It beats flute practice."

Jamie smiled. She stopped at the corner and squeezed Ann-Marie's arm. "I just want to say thanks," she said.

Ann-Marie looked surprised. It wasn't like Jamie to get mushy. "Thanks for what?"

"For believing me," Jamie said, suddenly embarrassed. She shook her long, black hair. "For believing me about everything that's happened."

"Well, of course I believe you," Ann-Marie said quickly.

"That's been real important to me," Jamie said, looking into the distance. "Because sometimes I haven't believed myself."

"Hey, Jamie! Take one and pass it on," Chris Hopping cried impatiently, shoving the exams toward Jamie.

"Oh. Sorry. Guess I was daydreaming." She took the papers and passed them to Laurie Weber in front of her.

"No, Jamie. You forgot to take one," Chris said. "Are you totally vegged out, or something?"

"No. I—yes. I mean—" She tapped Laurie on the shoulder and asked her for one of the exams back.

She had daydreamed her way through the entire school day, unable to concentrate on anything, unable to hear anything.

Tom hadn't been in homeroom. She realized that she was a little relieved about that. They wouldn't have been able to talk during school anyway.

Word had gotten around about Tom's dad being in a bad accident. But no one seemed to know any more than Jamie did about how he was doing or where Tom was.

A few kids asked her about it, but she could only tell them that she hadn't heard from Tom. Most of Jamie's friends saw that she was upset, that she had dark circles under her eyes and looked really tired and drawn, and so they kept their distance. They knew how close she was with Tom's family. They didn't want to make her uncomfortable or bother her for details.

And so she made it through most of the school day without having to talk to anyone. Around eleven-thirty, during Advanced Algebra, a storm came up outside. The sky turned an eerie green-black, and enormous rain droplets pounded the window. The rain was so heavy and loud that Mr. Andropolus, the algebra instructor, had to shout, straining his tiny, whistlelike voice to be heard.

Thunder roared nearby even though there was no lightning. The sky went from green-black to purple.

Jamie stared at the window, hypnotized by the sound of the pounding raindrops, by the splat of the big drops as they hit the windowpane and then cascaded down the glass in a thick, continuous stream.

She had a strong urge to run out of the room, to dash out into the rain, to let the big drops cover her, to feel the cold, refreshing water all over her body, to let the powerful rain wash her away, away from the school yard, away from Cloverhill, away from her life.

Then, as suddenly as it started, the rain stopped. The sky brightened and returned to gray. Robins chirped noisily in the trees outside the window. They swooped down to the grass to pull up the juicy worms the rain had drawn to the surface.

What a strange day, Jamie thought.

"I'll ask you one more time, Jamie. Earth calling Jamie. Are you there, Jamie?"

She slowly became aware that someone was repeating her name.

A few kids in the class were laughing, laughing at her.

She turned from the window.

"Earth calling Jamie. Do you read me?"

It was Mr. Andropolus. He had his hands cupped around his mouth like a megaphone. She guessed he'd been calling her for some time.

"Sorry," she said, feeling herself blush. "The rain. I was—uh—watching it."

"Luckily it stopped. Or we would still be robbed of the pleasure of your company," he said in his reedy little voice, grinning as if he'd just made the best joke ever made.

A few kids giggled, mostly nervous giggles.

"Sorry," Jamie repeated. She felt invaded. She had chosen to sit in the back row because she thought it would offer safety from being called on. But now she had been called on and embarrassed. Her remote seat hadn't protected her at all.

"Can you solve this for *X* and for *Y?*" Mr. Andropolus asked, pointing at a long equation he had written on the chalkboard.

"Uh, let me see," Jamie said, squinting hard at it.

The numbers and letters were all out of focus. It was just a white blur on the green background.

"I can't read it. My eyes. I—"

"What part can't you read, Jamie?" Mr. Andropolus asked, his tone becoming sympathetic.

"All of it," she admitted, blushing again. "I left my glasses at home. It's all just a blur to me."

"You try it then, David," Andropolus said, moving on to the boy next to her. "Is it a blur to you too?"

"No," David Conowitz said. He began to factor the equation.

All a blur, Jamie thought.

She looked around the large room and realized for the first time just how fuzzy and unclear everything looked to her when she didn't wear her glasses.

It's so soothing, she thought.

Living in a blur is so much more soothing, so much nicer than seeing the real world clearly. How nice it would be, she thought, to spend the rest of her life in a comfortable, warm blur.

The rest of the day seemed to go by just as she wished, a blur of faces, voices, papers being passed back and forth, noisy hallways, crashing locker doors. It seemed to take forever, and no time at all. In her own blur, shielded behind her dark thoughts, there was no time, and there was too much time.

Then suddenly the last bell had rung. She was piling books into her locker, and taking out her big, oversized green sweater. She started to pull it over her head, and then stopped. It was Tom's sweater. She had borrowed the sweater from him after a football game in the fall, and had never given it back. They used to joke about how it looked so much better on her.

Now she was going to wear it to turn him in to the police.

She held the sweater up, tried to picture him in it. But he had become a blur, too.

"Jamie, you can't put it on that way. You have to pull it over your head."

Jamie turned to find Ann-Marie, in a bright yellow rain slicker, standing behind her. "Very funny." She sighed and tossed the sweater back into the locker.

"How was your day?" Ann-Marie asked.

"I'm not sure," Jamie told her. "I really don't remember."

"So it was like every other day!" Ann-Marie cracked. "I had a run-in with Gibson in French this afternoon."

"Over what?"

"Pronunciation. What else? I get so sick of having to say everything in that class five times. Gibson thinks he can push everyone around because he's seven feet tall."

"So what'd you do?" Jamie asked.

"Punched him in the kneecaps, naturally!"

They both laughed.

"I finally got you to laugh," Ann-Marie said. "Are you still up for our visit to the police station?"

The smile faded quickly from Jamie's face. She nervously tossed her long, black hair back. "Yeah. I guess so."

Laura Patten walked by, holding hands with Steve Gurwin.

Jamie looked away. She stared down at the crumpled sweater in her locker. Tom and I used to walk around like that, she thought.

"Since when are they an item?" Ann-Marie whispered, after they had passed.

"I don't know," Jamie said absently.

"Isn't he a little young for her? He's only a junior."

"He was held back a year. He's our age," Jamie said, beginning to sound irritated. "Do we have to talk about Steve Gurwin?"

"Sorry. Sorry. Sorry," Ann-Marie said, taking a few steps back.

"I mean, this isn't easy for me. And once I tell the police what I saw and what's happened to me since, it's going to get even worse." Jamie leaned against the wall, holding on to the locker door as if she didn't ever want to let go of it.

"I said I was sorry," Ann-Marie said, pulling her arm. "Come on. Let's go. Let's get it over with."

Looking at the green sweater one last time, Jamie slammed the locker door shut.

They pushed open the wide double doors and stepped out of the main entrance. The storm had passed, leaving gray skies and steamy, thick air. The glass glistened. The sidewalks were still wet.

"Gross. It's like a steambath," Ann-Marie complained. "It's good you left that heavy sweater behind." She began to pull off her rain slicker.

"It's like walking in hot Jell-O," Jamie said. "That rain this morning—"

She stopped.

"Tom!" she cried.

He was across the street, leaning on the hood of a banged-up maroon van.

Where did he get the van?

"Tom!"

He stood up when he saw her waving to him.

"What?" Ann-Marie cried, struggling with the fasteners on the rain slicker. "Jamie, where are you going?"

But Jamie was already running across the street. "Finally!" she yelled to him. "You're finally back!"

He looked surprised. Then he grinned at her.

"Hey, Jamie, wait!"

She stopped in the middle of the street.

Another voice was calling to her. "Jamie, wait up!" Another boy's voice called from down the block.

Confused, she turned to see who it was.

And she saw *another Tom* running at full speed, desperately trying to catch up to her.

15

My nightmare—it's come true!

There are two Toms, and they're both coming after me.

But I'm not dreaming this. It's really happening.

The two Toms are real.

The two Toms are coming to smother me.

Jamie froze in the middle of the street. She was paralyzed by a blur of horrifying images, images from her nightmare mixed with what she was seeing now.

"Jamie, stop! Wait!" the Tom running down the street yelled.

Suddenly two strong hands roughly grabbed her arms just below the shoulders. "Let's go, babe," a voice—not Tom's voice—said, hot breath in her face. The two hands jerked her toward the back of the van.

The van door swung open. Jamie tried to pull away. But he was too strong for her. "In you go."

"No!" she screamed. "No!"

But he was lifting her into the back of the van.

Struggling to get out of his powerful grasp, she turned and looked into his face.

She saw immediately that he wasn't Tom.

It was another boy with white-blond hair. A boy with steel gray eyes. And a deep scar across his forehead and down his cheek. And thin, cruel lips twisted up into an excited grin.

"In you go, babes."

That voice. Yes. She recognized it. It was the voice from the threatening phone calls.

"Tom!" she screamed. "Tom! Help me!"

"Help! Somebody! Help!" She could hear Ann-Marie screaming from the school steps.

The screaming didn't seem to bother the gray-eyed boy who held her. He coolly picked her up and, with little effort, shoved her into the back of the van.

"Tom—"

The door slammed in her face.

She realized the engine was running.

She tried the back door. It was locked from the outside.

She turned to climb over the seat and escape through a side door. But she faced a solid wall. There was a steel partition between the trunk compartment and the back seat.

She was locked in. A caged animal.

This can't be happening. This is another nightmare, right?

"Let me out!" she screamed without realizing it. "Let me out! Let me out!"

She banged her fists against the front wall.

"Tom! Please!"

Was it the real Tom who had been running down the street calling her?

She turned and tried to force the solid back door open. She couldn't budge the handle. The only window in the back door was a small oval one, too small to escape through.

"Somebody! Please!"

She heard the driver's door slam shut.

A few seconds later she heard the tires squeal beneath her as the van pulled away.

"Ouch!"

She was thrown hard against the back door.

Struggling to her knees, she heard the engine roar as the van accelerated.

"Hey! Stop! Let me out!"

Such foolish, futile screaming.

But she had to do something.

The image of the two Toms flashed in her mind.

Again and again, her mind recreated the scarred, grinning face of the one who wasn't Tom.

The white wave of hair, that white-blond hair, the same length, the same color as Tom's.

The van swerved hard, tossing her against the side. Her arms ached where he had grabbed her so tightly and lifted her into this prison. Her throat felt dry and knotted. She was breathing hard and fast. It was so hot back here, so hot and uncomfortable.

Where was he taking her? What did he plan to do?

Who was he?

She began banging again on the steel barrier between her and the seats in front. "Stop! Let me out! Stop!"

A small door in the partition, a little bigger than a cigarette pack, slid open. She pressed her face against it and looked through.

He had one hand on the wheel, the other resting on the back of the seat. He was wearing a gray T-shirt. An unlit cigarette bobbed up and down on the side of his mouth.

He looked at her in the rearview mirror and grinned, pleased with himself.

"I told you you wouldn't get away," he said, and swerved the van onto the freeway.

16

"It's t-t-t-too bad you had to see me," he stammered, his cold gray eyes staring straight ahead at the highway. He shook his head, and repeated the words "too bad" over and over.

"This is a mistake. A big mistake," Jamie insisted.

"Too bad," he muttered. His odd, lopsided grin spread a little wider. When he smiled, the long scars on his face wrinkled.

He held the wheel with one hand and began to pound it rhythmically with the other, tapping and pounding to a beat only he could hear.

Jamie became aware of everything. In her fear, in her panic, she felt as if all of her senses had been heightened. She could hear the rumble of the van's engine as it shifted gears, hear the tires roll over the pavement. She smelled the stale aroma of cigarette smoke in the torn vinyl seat cushions. The pungent aroma of overripe fruit drifted up from the floor beneath the front seat.

Her eyes seemed to take in twice as much as normal. She peered through the tiny opening in the steel partition as if looking into a microscope.

She saw the crack in the windshield that ran diagonally from the center down across the passenger's side. She saw neat rows of cigarette burns across the tan vinyl dashboard. Someone had very carefully, very methodically burned small black circles in the dash.

She saw the brand name printed on the cigarette behind the young man's ear. She saw the sunlight glinting off the big ruby-colored glass in the center of the ring he wore on his right hand, the hand that tapped the wheel harder and faster as he drove.

She saw the open glove compartment, saw a pair of black leather gloves inside, stuffed in with maps and other papers. She saw a long white rope coiled on the front seat, the kind of rope victims on TV crime shows always get tied up with.

She saw every detail, smelled every smell, heard every sound as if all the volume and picture controls on a TV had been set up as far and as loud and as bright as they could go.

Everything had been a blur all day. But now, even without her glasses, she could see perfectly. If only she could return to the warm safety of the blur . . .

If only she could think of something to help her escape . . .

"It's too bad you had to see me," he repeated suddenly. "I could tell that you recognized me too."

"No. No, I didn't!" Jamie screamed through the little opening. "I didn't recognize you."

His jaw tightened. He glanced into the rearview mirror, then back at the highway. He tapped his ring rapidly against the steering wheel.

Jamie could tell they were going very fast, well beyond the 55 mph speed limit.

The police! A policeman will pull him over, she thought. No hope was too desperate. She listened for a siren. But there was only the rush of the wind and the steady roar of the tires against the pavement.

"How'd you recognize me?" he asked, looking at her in the rearview mirror, his eyes blank like solid gray marbles. "From my p-p-picture in the paper?"

"I don't know who you are," Jamie cried. "Please, you've got to believe me. I've never seen you. You've got the wrong person. If you'll just let me go, I won't tell anyone. I won't—"

He deliberately jerked the van hard to the right, forcing Jamie to fall backward. She struggled back to her knees, leaned forward and peered again through the small opening.

"From my picture in the paper?" he repeated. "From when I k-k-killed those idiots in that housing project?"

Killed?

Why did his smile grow wider when he said that word? How could he say it with such pride?

"I don't know who you are," Jamie said, her voice

surprisingly steady. "I don't know why you're picking on me. I have no idea who you are or what you want. I've never seen you before in my life."

He tossed back his head and laughed really hard, revealing two rows of yellow teeth. "Nice try, babes," he said, swerving the van to avoid hitting two motorcyclists in the left lane.

"Listen to me—" Jamie started.

"Nice try. But no go," he said. "I saw you in the jewelry store."

The words sent a shiver through her whole body. For a second, she felt sick. It passed quickly. She struggled to regain her composure, to keep control, to hold back the tears, the hysteria.

"I haven't been in any jewelry store," she said quietly. "You've got the wrong person."

He smiled at her in the rearview mirror, his scars creasing red and deep. He reached for something on the seat with his right hand, and held it up. "Then how'd I get this?" he asked.

Her wallet.

The sick feeling returned. She felt dizzy. She pressed her head against the metal van wall.

"I don't know you," she said weakly.

"Well, then I'd better introduce myself," he said. "I don't know where my manners have g-g-got to. I'm Okie Farnum. Now d'you remember me from all the papers?"

Okie Farnum. Okie Farnum.

Yes. It was a big story about three years before. He had killed an entire family, somewhere on the other side of town. She couldn't remember why. But it was a big story because he was just seventeen at the time. He was seventeen and not the least bit remorseful.

Jamie remembered that he'd been tried as an adult, even though he was still a juvenile.

"No. I don't remember you," she lied.

He looked disappointed.

"I've been in prison a while," he said, concentrating on passing another van.

That's right. Jamie remembered. He'd been sentenced to life imprisonment. And when he'd stood up in court and heard the verdict, he'd just grinned. He refused to look sorry. He refused to give anyone the satisfaction of seeing him look humble or defeated.

Seventeen and sentenced to life in prison, and he didn't even look sorry.

"But they couldn't hold me," he said. He laughed to himself. "No one can hold me for long."

Taptaptaptap. He continued to pound the big ring against the steering wheel.

I've got to get out! Jamie told herself, looking desperately for something to use to open the door, something to help her—anything!

But the back of the van had been completely cleaned out. And she couldn't reach anything on the other side of the metal partition.

It was so hot back there, so sticky. She tried to take deep breaths, but the air was stale and unpleasant. She gasped, and forced back the feeling that she was going to start screaming at the top of her lungs.

"You know, I really didn't think anyone would

recognize me," he was saying, staring at her in the rearview mirror.

"But I didn't. Really—" she protested weakly.

"Especially with this fake blond hair. Y'know how long it took me to dye it this funny white color?"

Jamie sank to the floor of the van. Feelings of guilt washed over her, nearly drowning out her fear.

How could I have suspected Tom?

How could I have been so disloyal?

This—criminal—dyed his hair white. And because of that, I was ready to turn Tom in to the police.

"I made a mistake. I thought you were someone else—my boyfriend," she called through the tiny opening. "I didn't know it was you. I don't care if you believe me or not. But that's the truth."

"Too late now," came his reply, followed by bitter laughter.

"Why? What are you going to do to me?" Jamie asked, her voice trembling.

"K-k-kill you, of course."

17

She didn't talk to him after that.

She slumped down to the floor of the van and waited in silence. She tried to think of an escape plan, but discovered she was too frightened to think clearly.

Pictures popped in and out of her mind. Strange pictures, real and unreal, not related to anything that was happening to her.

She saw Casey pleading with her to play Hungry Hippos. She saw Tom swimming in his first swim meet. She saw Ann-Marie suspended upside down by her ankles from the rings in the gym, smiling and swinging back and forth.

The mind acts so crazily, she thought, when you're about to die.

"Here we are, babes."

The van squealed to a stop.

Jamie heard the driver's door open. She looked

through the small opening. On the other side of the cracked windshield, she saw woods.

She heard Okie's footsteps crunching on gravel.

Suddenly the back door of the van was pulled open. The air outside was as stifling as inside the van. The sky was still a solid, dark gray.

Jamie saw a small stucco cabin on the edge of thick woods. For some reason, the cabin had been painted a pastel green. A woodshed, also pastel green, stood down a short dirt path from the cabin. A clothesline had been strung between tree trunks. Some socks and a pair of faded blue jeans hung drying on the line.

Okie had the long coil of rope in one hand. He reached into the van and grabbed Jamie's hand. "Here we go," he said, his gray eyes filled with menace.

He pulled her roughly out of the van and threw her to the gravel. "Hey!" she cried out, more in surprise than pain.

He pulled her to her feet and gave her a hard shove toward the cabin. "Get inside—quick," he said.

Jamie started slowly toward the small cabin. But she heard a cry. She turned back just in time to see Tom leap from the top of the van.

"What the—" Okie cried, astonished, as Tom landed on his shoulders, knocking him to the gravel.

For a brief second, Jamie thought she was dreaming again.

Two Toms grappled in the stony drive, two heads of white-blond hair, four arms punching and pushing, two heads grunting, crying out, groaning from pain and the exertions of the fight.

But it was no dream.

She quickly figured out that Tom must have leaped onto the back of the van before it pulled away from the front of the school. Then he must have held on for dear life all the way out to the woods.

Tom was on his back now, Okie riding on his chest, landing hard punches to his face. Forgetting her terror, forgetting how unreal the fight looked to her, Jamie ran forward and shoved Okie off Tom. Okie groaned loudly and rolled on the gravel.

Now Tom leaped on top of him, landing hard on Okie's stomach, causing him to cry out and gasp for breath.

"Run, Jamie! Run!" Tom called.

Jamie stood staring at the two white-blond heads, unable to move. This isn't happening, she thought. I'm imagining this, too.

"Jamie, run to the woods!"

Tom's desperate plea snapped her back to reality.

She turned and started toward the cabin.

No. Wrong way.

She looked back at the fight. Both of them were rolling in the gravel, struggling to get the advantage.

She looked for a tree limb, something to hit Okie with.

"No!" Tom shouted. "Run! Just run! Run and get help!"

Of course. She could get help. She could find another cabin down the road, or a gas station, or something. She could call the police. Yes. Get help.

But first she'd have to get away.

If she headed for the road, it would be easy for Okie to catch up to her. Tom was right. She had to run to the woods.

She could hear the grunts and cries of the fight as she ran over the tall weeds into the trees. The air felt thick and wet. It seemed to get even hotter as she ran over the thick brambles, twigs and tree limbs, and tangles of tall weeds still wet from the rain.

The ground was soft and marshy. She ran stooped over, with her arms in front of her face, shielding herself from thorny branches and low limbs that seemed to swing up at her from out of nowhere.

Running blindly, she tried to keep parallel to the road and hoped that the woods ended at someone's property line, that she'd soon come to a cabin or farmhouse where she could get help. She cried aloud when something scampered past her feet. But she quickly realized that it was just a rabbit she had startled.

"Bet I'm more scared than you are," she told the rabbit as she ran over a thick carpet of pine needles.

Past the pine needles, her heart pounding, her throat too dry to swallow, a pain in her side spreading around to her chest. Through low, thick bushes. Into a muddy clearing.

With a loud sloshing sound, the mud rose up over her sneakers. She pulled her knees high, trying to float over the mud, and realized that her left sneaker had come untied.

Should she stop to tie it?

If she did, Okie might catch up to her.

If she didn't, it might come off in the mud.

She turned, looked behind her, listened. No sounds. No one coming.

She bent over to tie her sneaker, the muddy laces slipping through her fingers. It seemed to take forever. The pain in her side grew sharper. She couldn't see clearly enough to hold the laces.

Finally she had them tied. She stood up, started to run across the small clearing—and tripped over someone's raised white boot.

"Where y'all off to, honey?"

Jamie scampered quickly up from the mud. She turned to see that she had been tripped by a tall, thin woman with bleached red hair piled up in a bun on top of her heavily made-up face. The woman wore ragged jean cutoffs, a bright blue and green bowling shirt and white plastic boots.

"Don't be in such a hurry. That ain't neighborly," she said.

She rushed forward, grabbed Jamie's right arm, and jerked it behind her.

"Ow! Stop! You're hurting me!" Jamie cried, struggling unsuccessfully to get out of the tall woman's grasp.

"Okie'd be real unhappy if you slipped away," the woman said. "And you don't wanna make Okie unhappy, do you, honey? I'm Okie's girl, and take it from me, dear, you don't ever wanna make Okie unhappy."

Twisting Jamie's arm behind her, the woman turned her around and began to force her back toward the cabin.

18

What's going on?" Tom whispered. His left eye was swollen nearly shut. Blood trickled from his nose and from a cut on his right cheek.

"It's a long story," Jamie whispered, looking at Okie and his girlfriend Dolly as they discussed things on the other side of the tiny, one-room cabin.

Tom and Jamie were side by side on low wooden chairs, tied with their hands behind them. They had both struggled to free themselves at first, but the ropes wouldn't budge. They gave up, sat quietly, each trapped in fear of what would happen next, watching Okie pace the small cabin.

"It's b-b-b-bath time," Okie was saying, pointing to the rusted metal bathtub in the far corner of the room. "What choice do I have, Doll? I've got no other choice."

Bath time?

What did he mean by that?

Jamie shuddered as she suddenly remembered. Okie had killed that family by *drowning* them! He had told the judge that drowning was such a clean way to die.

Tom looked at Jamie and tried to force an encouraging smile. But his face was too swollen and bloody. He couldn't manage it.

Dolly came over and wiped a dirty handkerchief across Tom's bleeding cheek. She looked down at them and shook her head sympathetically.

"You look like nice kids," she said with sincere regret. "Too bad you had to recognize Okie. He just can't go back to that prison. He's too sensitive."

Okie angrily kicked an empty beer can across the floor. "You heard her," he said, frowning. "I'm too sensitive. Too bad. Too bad."

"Just let us go," Jamie said. "You'll never hear from us again. We won't say a word to anybody."

Okie laughed and kicked another beer can. This one flew up and landed in the small stainless steel sink.

"It's all a mistake," Jamie insisted. "I thought you were my boyfriend, see. Because of your hair. Look at his hair. It's the same color as yours, and so I thought—"

"Shut up!" Okie screamed, raising his arm and rushing at Jamie, ready to hit her.

He stopped a few feet away and turned to Dolly. "She's giving me a headache," he complained, suddenly sounding like a little kid.

She walked over beside him and began to massage his temples with her long, skinny fingers. He lowered his head and stood still, enjoying the massage.

"That's great, Doll. That's it. That's great. You sure know how to calm Okie down. I always get a little t-t-t-tense . . . before bath time."

"You're just so sensitive, Okie," she said soothingly, her bright pink fingernails moving slowly across his temple. "That's your whole problem, ya know."

"Do my neck," he said. He turned, and she began to rub the back of his neck and knead his narrow shoulders.

Tom and Jamie silently worked at loosening their ropes. But it was hopeless.

"What do we do now?" Jamie whispered.

Tom shrugged, grimacing in pain. "We'll have to wait for him to untie us," he whispered. "Then try to get out the door and into the woods." He didn't sound very hopeful.

"I'm so sorry," Jamie whispered. "So sorry."

Dolly finished her massage and backed away from Okie. "Thanks, Doll," he said, rolling his head around loosely on his neck. "That feels much better. Guess I'll run the tub."

He walked across the room to the tub in the corner, leaned over, resting one hand on the wall, and turned on both faucets full force. "Gotta do this f-f-f-fast," he stammered. "Someone may have seen the van at her school. We've gotta make tracks."

"I'm all packed up, hon," Dolly said. She picked up

a battered yellow suitcase by its broken handle. "Shall I put this in the van?"

"No. Later. I might need your help with these two."

"Aw, Okie, you know I can't stand to watch." She made a face, her bright red lipsticked lips forming a pout.

"Tub's full," he muttered, turning off the faucets. "You don't have to watch, Doll. But I may need you to help me hold 'em down. They're both pretty frisky when they want to be." He rubbed his jaw, which was cut and swollen from one of Tom's punches.

"Let's do him first," Okie said, closing his gray eyes and stretching his arms as if preparing for some kind of gymnastic event.

Jamie wasn't sure if Tom knew what Okie planned to do. "He's going to drown us," she whispered.

"No!" Tom's swollen face contorted in fear. "No! Please!"

Okie, wiping off his hands with a dirty dish towel, grinned at them. "It don't take long," he said. "Unless you put up a struggle."

"But this is all unnecessary," Jamie pleaded, her voice high and shrill. "You can just let us go. We'll never tell anyone about this. Never!"

"I know you won't," Okie said, tossing the towel to Dolly.

"Don't toy with them, hon. Just do it and let's get outta here," Dolly said, sounding nervous, even afraid.

"Can't you reason with him?" Jamie begged Dolly.

"Can't you convince him that he doesn't have to do this?"

Dolly looked at her with real sadness. "Okie's real sensitive," she said softly. "He knows what he's got to do. I never tell Okie what to do."

"That's right, babes." Okie looked at her with pride.

"I know where you can get some money," Tom interrupted, unable to hide the fear and desperation from his trembling voice. "Lots of money. Let us go and I'll take you there."

Okie shook his head. "Don't ever try to kid a kidder, boy," he said quietly. Then his face filled with anger. "I *t-t-told* you it don't take long!"

He took a knife from the wooden table beside the sink, walked up behind Tom and cut the ropes. He kept the knife in Tom's back, and pulled Tom up by the hair with the other hand.

"Hey—" Tom shouted weakly.

"No! No!" Jamie yelled at the top of her lungs.

Dolly rushed over and jammed the wet dish towel into Jamie's mouth.

Jamie's cries continued, muffled by the towel, as she watched Okie shove Tom over to the bathtub. Pressing the knife into Tom's back, Okie forced Tom to get down on his knees beside the metal tub.

Frozen in horror, Jamie wanted to turn away. But she couldn't. She had to keep watching until . . . until Tom broke free and escaped. Until Okie changed his mind. . . . Until a miracle happened. . . .

"No! Wait!" Tom cried.

But Okie pulled him up by his hair, pressing the knife into his back.

Tom flailed out with his arms.

But he hit only air.

"No! You can't! Please! No!"

Okie slid his hand down the back of Tom's head—and pushed.

Tom's head went into the water with a loud splash.

He tried to kick at Okie. He tried to push him away. He squirmed and wiggled and tossed his whole body.

But Okie held tight and pushed Tom's head farther under the water.

Tom struggled for a while longer. Then his body seemed to deflate.

He slumped over the side of the tub. His arms dropped to his sides.

Okie dropped the knife and raised his wrist so he could see his watch. Holding Tom's head under the water with one hand, he stared at the watch on his other arm, his face a blank, expressionless, unconcerned.

Jamie lowered her head and closed her eyes. She couldn't bear to watch Tom's limp, unmoving body any longer. Tears poured down her face. Her loud sobs were muffled by the wet towel in her mouth.

"There. That should do it," she heard Okie say finally. "Exactly three minutes."

He sounded almost cheerful.

19

Please, please. Let me be crazy.

Let this all be in my head.

I imagined the whole thing.

Let me open my eyes, and it will all be gone. I'll be back in my room, waiting for Tom.

Please, please. Don't let him be drowned in that horrid bathtub.

Make this cabin disappear.

Make these dreadful people just a dream, another nightmare.

Jamie couldn't stop crying. And thinking.

And praying.

Why should Tom die? It was all her fault, all her stupid mistake. He was only trying to rescue her. He didn't know who these people were. He didn't know why Jamie had been kidnapped. He didn't know anything.

So why should Tom die?

He shouldn't die.

He *can't* die.

Please, please, please. He can't die.

But when she opened her eyes and forced herself to see through her tears, Tom hadn't moved. He was still on his knees, his body draped over the side of the tub, his head in the water, unmoving, still, his arms hanging limp at his sides, his palms flat and lifeless against the wooden floorboards.

"Sorry, honeybunch. You're next."

Dolly's words, spoken softly from right above Jamie, didn't register. Jamie didn't even hear them.

Her shoulders heaved from her silent sobs. She choked on the towel. Dolly pulled it out until Jamie stopped choking. Then she quickly stuffed it back in.

Okie, holding the knife again, stepped toward Dolly, a thoughtful expression on his face. "I've got an idea, Doll," he said, looking down at Jamie.

"Yes, hon?"

"Well, she's such a pretty thing," Okie said slowly, reluctantly, "can't we keep her with us—you know, as a slave or something?"

Dolly stomped her boot against the floor. "Okie—no."

He looked hurt.

"I'm only thinking of you, Sugar Doll. I'll bet she'd be a good, hard worker. She could do the cleaning and cooking, all the work, and you could sit back and take it easy and just enjoy life."

"I already enjoy life," Dolly said loudly. Then she quickly softened her tone, obviously afraid to anger or cross Okie. "And you know I enjoy working for you, Okie. It ain't work if it's for you. It's a pleasure." She walked up and kissed him behind the ear.

Okie looked back at Jamie, who was sobbing quietly, listening to every word but looking down at the floor.

"I still think she could come in real handy," he insisted, sounding peevish.

"I know what you're thinking," Dolly scolded.

He shook his head. "No, that ain't it. I just think it would be real n-n-nice to have a servant. You know, be like rich folks."

"Now, Okie, stop and think a minute," Dolly said softly. "You've got to realize she'll only be trouble. No matter where we took her and how well we treated her, she'd try to escape the first chance she got. We'd have to be on guard duty twenty-four hours a day. Now, that wouldn't be no fun, would it?"

Okie thought about it for a long time.

It seemed like an eternity to Jamie.

Tell her you want to keep me alive, she thought.

Tell her you want to keep me around to do all the work.

Tell her you want a slave, you creep. You creep!

Tell her.

Tell her.

I just want to stay alive.

I just want to stay alive long enough to pay you back for drowning Tom.

"I guess you're right, Doll," Okie said, rubbing his sore jaw. "I guess you're right, as always."

"I'm always right for you, hon," Dolly said, pleased with herself. "You know I always do right for you." She smoothed a hand up over the red hair piled high on her head.

He stepped toward Jamie, raised the knife and cut away the ropes.

Jamie looked up. Looked beyond Okie. Looked at the figure coming up behind Okie.

Her eyes bulged wide in disbelief.

The wet dish towel fell to her lap as her mouth opened in shock.

Dolly turned and followed Jamie's astonished gaze.

"But—but you're *dead!*" Dolly shrieked.

20

Tom moved forward quickly, his eyes revealing more fear than anger, water running down his face, dripping from his hair. He ran up behind Okie, who still hadn't turned around, who still had no idea why Jamie was looking beyond him.

Tom raised a broom handle high in the air and brought it down hard on Okie's head.

Okie dodged to the side at the last second.

The broom handle missed his head and crashed down onto his shoulder. A loud *craaaack* shattered the silence of the small cabin.

Okie screamed in surprise, and, grabbing his shoulder, spun around to face his attacker.

"No!" he cried, his face contorted in pain, his scars a vivid scarlet. "No! You're dead! You're dead!"

Holding his broken shoulder, he lurched forward, stabbing at Tom with the knife in his hand.

Tom leaped aside, easily avoiding Okie's desperate stabs. He swung the broom handle like a baseball bat, smashing it hard into Okie's hand. The knife flew across the room.

Okie cried out in pain, clutching his shoulder with his one good hand. Then, moving with surprising speed, he lunged forward and tore the broom handle from Tom's grasp.

With a desperate scream, Dolly dived across the room for the knife.

Jamie pulled herself free from the ropes, and dived after Dolly. She grabbed Dolly's legs in a flying tackle. Dolly cried out in surprise and frustration.

Dolly rolled onto her back, grabbed Jamie's long hair in both hands and pulled. Jamie screamed in pain and tried to pull away from Dolly's grip. She swung at Dolly's face with her fists until Dolly let go.

Then Jamie leaped to her feet, and tried to land a hard kick in Dolly's midsection. But Dolly quickly scrambled out of the way, and the kick went wild, throwing Jamie off balance.

Jamie looked around the cabin desperately for a weapon, for anything she could use.

Dolly turned back to her with a grin on her face. She had the knife in her hand.

Jamie started to back up. But Dolly leaped at her, swinging the knife down hard.

Jamie screamed as Dolly tripped over one of the low, wooden chairs. The knife hit the floor first and bounced away.

Dolly's head hit the corner of the wooden table as she fell. She slumped to the floor in a heap.

And didn't get up.

Jamie crawled to the knife, grasped it tightly, climbed to her feet and held it over Dolly.

But she didn't need to.

Dolly was unconscious.

Jamie stood staring down at Dolly for a second or two. The sound of Tom's cries made her spin around. Okie had Tom's head in both hands and was smashing it against the side of the bathtub.

Without thinking, Jamie threw the knife with all her might.

The blade flew into the back of Okie's already broken shoulder. He howled in pain and turned away from Tom, struggling to pull the blade free.

Tom rolled away from him, retrieved the broom handle and brought it down hard on Okie's head.

Okie uttered a last groan and slumped to the floor, unconscious.

Jamie ran to Tom. She suddenly realized she was laughing and crying at the same time.

"Tom!"

A second later, she was in his arms.

He pulled her close and hugged her. He was dripping wet, but she didn't care. He was real. He was alive.

They kissed.

They stood in the middle of the cabin holding each other.

She felt that if she ever let go of him, he would disappear again, become a dream, a lost dream.

But holding on to him so tightly, she realized that her dreams—their dreams—could begin again. The nightmare had ended.

After a long while, he pulled back, still holding her hands. He shook his head hard, shaking off water like a dog.

They both laughed.

"You see a towel anywhere?" he asked.

She had too many tears in her eyes to see anything.

"Thank heavens for Coach Daniels and his breath control practices!" Tom said, squeezing her hands. "I'll never complain again about all the times he forced us to hold our breath underwater for four minutes!"

"I—I guess it came in handy," Jamie said, forcing a smile. The picture of Tom struggling as Okie pushed his head underwater flashed back into her mind. And once again she saw him draped lifelessly over the side, his limp arms hanging down, his hands flat on the floorboards.

She shuddered and pulled him close again.

"You're real," she whispered. "You are real, aren't you?"

Okie groaned down on the floor, startling them both.

"Quick," Tom said, pulling away. "The ropes."

They picked up the ropes from the floor. "Help

me," Tom said, beginning to tie Okie's hands behind him.

Jamie rolled Dolly onto her stomach and started to tie her hands. Tying people up always looked so easy on TV. But it was harder than it looked, she decided, especially when your hands were shaking, when you were trembling all over, when the tears wouldn't stop rolling from your eyes.

"Who are your friends here?" Tom asked, tying Okie's ankles now.

Jamie sighed. "It's such a long story. Such a long, horrible story."

He smiled at her reassuringly. "You don't have to tell me if you don't want."

"No. I want to," she cried. "I have to. This was all my fault. All my fault."

He came over to help her finish tying up Dolly. "Yeah. I guess you owe me one," he said, concentrating on the rope. "Now, start at the beginning. Where did you meet this fun couple?"

"I didn't," she said. "I mean, I only met Okie. Except I didn't meet him."

"This *is* going to be a long story!" He laughed, then kissed her on the cheek. He could see how upset she was. Despite the horror he had been through, he was trying to calm her, to help her get over it all.

"It started Saturday afternoon," she said, deciding to plunge right into it. "When you didn't show up for our skating date, I went to the mall with Ann-Marie."

"Oh. So actually, this is all *my* fault for not showing up," Tom said, getting to his feet.

"Well, sort of." She thought about it for a second. "Yeah. I guess it *is* your fault."

Tom leaned over and started searching through the pockets of Okie's jeans. Okie groaned but didn't open his eyes.

"What are you doing?"

"Looking for the keys to the van. We've got to take it and get to a phone. Maybe this time I'll ride inside instead of on the back!"

"Here they are." She picked them up off the wooden table.

"Let's go," he said, pulling her out the door. The sun had gone down behind the trees. The night air was still hot and wet. "You can tell me the rest of the story on the way."

They climbed into the front of the van. Tom started the engine and backed down the gravel drive.

"At the mall, Ann-Marie and I split up," she told him, as they pulled onto the highway. "I went into a jewelry store, the Diamond Ranch. I saw a holdup taking place. The robber had a gun. He shot the store owner. It was Okie. But from where I was hiding, I saw his denim jacket, and his hair . . . and . . ."

"You thought it was me?"

She turned toward the window. "Yes," she whispered.

He laughed. "You thought *I* was robbing a jewelry store?" He thought it was hilarious. "Jamie, you *know* how nearsighted you are without your glasses. And you weren't wearing them, *were* you?"

"Well, no . . ." she said weakly. "But he looked just like you. And I didn't know where you were. You had never broken a date before, and—"

"I couldn't have been robbing a jewelry store," he said, still laughing, "because I was across town robbing a bank instead!"

"You're not funny," she said, refusing to laugh, staring out the window.

When he stopped laughing, she turned back to him. "You know, you have some explaining to do, too. Where were you Saturday afternoon? Andy said you left early. He said you weren't in the locker room after swim practice. And then Saturday night at the dance, in the wood shop, you really scared me. You were acting so strange, pacing back and forth with that metal pick."

His expression turned serious. "I didn't mean to scare you. I was just real nervous."

"What was it you wanted to tell me?"

"I wanted to tell you that I made a decision during swim practice. I left the pool early. I got dressed and I waited in Coach Daniels's office. I guess that's why Andy didn't see me."

"But why?"

"I wanted to talk to Coach Daniels. I quit the swim team."

"You *what?*"

"Quit the swim team. It was taking up too much of

my time. I decided I needed to get an after-school job instead. My family really needs the money. Especially now, with my dad having a long recuperation ahead of him."

"And Saturday night in the wood shop—"

"I was just so nervous about telling you I quit the team. I knew you'd be very disappointed. I guess that's why I acted so strange."

"And the gold earrings? I—I thought you had taken them during the holdup."

Tom laughed. "I've been saving up for nearly a year to buy those. I wanted to save them as a graduation present for you. But then I felt bad about Saturday night. So I decided to give them to you early. I wanted you to have them as soon as you woke up on Sunday morning."

He pulled off the highway into a little gas station. The station was dark and closed, but there was a phone booth to the side of the pumps where they could call the police.

Jamie shook her head, still trying to get everything clear in her mind. "You wanted to tell me you'd quit the swim team—and I thought you wanted to tell me that you'd murdered someone!"

He reached across the car seat and patted her shoulder. "I think that's what they call a small breakdown in communication," he said.

She took his hand and held it tightly. "I have an idea to keep us out of trouble from now on," she said. "I'll make a promise if you'll make a promise."

"Let's hear yours first. What's your promise?"

"Never to go out again without wearing my glasses."

"That sounds good. And what's my promise?" he asked.

"Never to break another date!"

ABOUT THE AUTHOR

R. L. STINE is the author of more than twenty mysteries and thrillers for Young Adult readers. He also writes funny novels and joke books.

In addition to his publishing work, he is Head Writer of the children's TV show "Eureeka's Castle."

He lives in New York City with his wife, Jane, and son Matt.